Thomas Bulen Jacobs
CYBERSCION
Neon Hemlock Press

advance praise for
CYBERSCION

"*Cyberscion*'s neon-slick setting and lovable cast of characters lured me in from the start, while the story's emotional heart—conflict between tradition and upheaval—kept me hooked."
—Dominique Dickey, author of *Redundancies and Potentials*

"A thrilling and kinetic cyberheist, pulled off by a queer crew I wish I could hire to solve all my problems, full of delicious meals, cyber-topology, expected betrayals, and unexpected loyalty."
—Ann LeBlanc, author of *The Transitive Properties of Cheese*

"*Cyberscion* is a delight, with engrossing worldbuilding, vivid characters, and a plot brimming with cyberpunk twists and turns. Jacobs delivers a heist narrative that's propulsive, erudite, occasionally steamy, and always captivating."
—Izzy Wasserstein, author of *All the Hometowns You Can't Stay Away From*

"*Cyberscion* is everything *Star Wars* should be; painting a vivid, multicultural future in a short amount of time, with a scrappy cast you will love."
—TT Madden, author of *The Cosmic Color*

"...cyberpunk fans will find this a fast-paced, action-packed romp with plenty to hold their attention."
—*Publishers Weekly*

Neon Hemlock Press
www.neonhemlock.com
@neonhemlock

© 2026 Thomas Bulen Jacobs

Cyberscion
Thomas Bulen Jacobs

All rights reserved. No part of this publication may be reproduced, stored in a retrieval system or transmitted in any form or by any means, electronic, mechanical, photocopying, recording or otherwise without the prior permission of the publisher or in accordance with the provisions of the Copyright, Designs and Patents Act 1988 or under the terms of any license permitting limited copying issued by the Copyright Licensing Agency.

This novella is entirely a work of fiction. Names, characters, places and incidents are the products of the author's imagination or are used fictitiously. Any resemblance to actual events, locales, organizations or persons, living or dead, is entirely coincidental.

Cover Illustration by DOFRESH
Interior Design and Layout by dave ring
Edited by dave ring

Print ISBN-13: 978-1-966503-20-0
Ebook ISBN-13: 978-1-966503-21-7

CYBERSCION

THOMAS BULEN JACOBS

For Brianne.

Always and in every way for you.

One

Benjiro Ibn Benjiro Ayad Nakamura, scion of clan Nakamura, heir apparent to the regency of the cybersinecure of Manahatta, had never stepped foot in the outerboroughs.

To think that now he was doing so to meet a thief.

The driverless VTOL cab descended at its secret coordinates at the appointed time and deposited him precisely where they wanted him to be. The rotor blades stilled, then folded noiselessly back like the wings of a cicada. There was a slight hiss, and the door slid up and back. Ben remained seated for a moment. Bracing himself, he descended to the pavement.

Unweighted, the cab unfolded its shimmering rotors and alighted quickly. Ben bent his head to watch it go. As it passed, the yellow vacancy indicator light blinked on. His connection to Manahatta was truly severed.

So be it.

Ben turned to get his bearings. He was dressed as he had assumed the plebeians would be, in black trousers and blazer. He wore a shimmering black silk shirt with a Mandarin collar clasped with jade. His long black hair was bound at the back of his head in a high tight topknot. His beard, inherited from his mother's side, was dark and trim.

What he found, standing on a busy corner in Queensborough, betrayed his expectations so thoroughly that he chafed at the defiance of the colors he saw around him: canary Kente; tart cherry dashiki; robin's egg kimonos like those his sisters wore to the convocations of the clans.

Ben was unnoticed, or at least unremarked upon. This too surprised him. He felt certain that he should be immediately recognized. With the ascension coming, his face gazed out from every holoboard and electric bus stop in the sinecure. Yet only a few of the faces glanced his way. He found them flat, broad, dry. His servants' faces were not so creased, so defiantly unrefined.

He had not expected to wait, another unfamiliar feeling, for in his milieu he had only to murmur a whim to have it gratified. He saw that he had absent-mindedly meandered down the block, and now hurried back, afraid of being missed.

He looked about again, anxious that he had been dropped off in the wrong place, or, worse, left here as chum for some nefarious plan. Above him was the vast crumbling underbelly of the old NRW subway tracks, the steel lattice stretching like a cobweb across the city. Teenagers in bright yellow and green jackets lounged across the nearby stairs smoking a hookah. It was pleasant, vanilla and tobacco. Against his better judgment, he found himself relaxing.

Kitty corner he could make out a Ramen shop, the name, Hokkaido Ramen, stenciled on the window in English and Japanese. There was a yerba maté hutch, hardly bigger than a window, serving a trickle of customers. Beside it, an empty shoe store, then a restaurant selling something called "empanadas." Down the street he could make out a public pharmacy, its green neon bright in the crepuscular light.

He tapped his watch. Five minutes had elapsed. He grew frustrated.

Then, as if in answer to his impatience, there came from overhead a cacophonous wrenching clatter. There was a metallic screech, a hiss and a shudder, and then in an instant, the world was drained of all sound. Ben whipped his head from side to side. No one else reacted to the awful grinding. He raised his gaze and was struck full in the face by a blast of acrid heat.

A thick black cord tumbled through a crevice in the floor of the station overhead. A moment later a figure slipped imperturbably down the rope. It wore a skintight black bodysuit, over which was clasped a black armored vest. Its face was hooded, a metal-tentacled breathing apparatus where the mouth should be, twin red orbs over eyes which scanned him sightlessly.

The figure's hands moved.

"Benjiro Nakamura." The voice was garbled, arachnoid.

He nodded. In an instant, the figure had taken him by the shoulders, twisted him about, and placed an arm across his chest. Then, somehow, they were lifted off the ground. Ben gasped to find himself pulled effortlessly up through the crevice in the overhang and deposited gently onto the platform, where there waited for them, carriage-like, a single battered subway car.

The bug—for the figure resembled nothing so much as an enormous insect—moved quickly, searching every pocket and crevice of his body. It removed his watch and phone, disabled both with a thin gold-tipped stylus, and secreted them into the utility belt around its waist. Ben had known this was coming. It didn't make the insolence—the effortlessness—of it any easier to bear.

"Get in," instructed the bug. Again, the strange contortions of the hands.

One of the subway car's doors was open, and Ben entered. The bug followed. Once aboard, it passed into the front of the car, where the control panel lived. Ben called after it, but the bug did not even acknowledge him.

Ben watched the bug move. It was tall, graceful. It? He? She? Impossible to tell. Broad-chested and soft hipped. Ben knew already its incredible strength. Yet it moved with a fluidity almost in defiance of gravity. He was startled by the sudden announcement through the empty air of the subway car: "Stand clear of the closing doors."

The door closed with a hydraulic hiss and the train lurched. Ben's knees gave out under him and he stumbled backwards into the orange plastic bucket seat behind him.

The subway car moved as though in an extended fall, careening ever faster and deeper into the vastness of Queensborough. For several minutes they remained above ground, but then, without warning, the train veered off into the underground. Ben caught snatches of signs, station names, scratched and faded to illegibility. Meaningless to him, at any rate.

Ben endured the journey in silence. The subway system had been shut down decades ago, a foul, inefficient and expensive relic of the old city. That it had been jerry-rigged to work now, against the laws of both the sinecure and technological progress, caused him to bristle once again.

But he had spent a lifetime training himself in the art of being dispassionate, so he interrogated this feeling. Why should he care what they did in the outerboroughs?

The answer was clear: someone, somewhere, was lying. Whether they were lying to him, or someone much further down the chain of information, was immaterial. How could he be expected to preside over the sinecure without accurate information? A misstep in ignorance would reverberate for years. He wondered whether his father knew of this kind of breach, whether he elided it as the small price of lubricating the gears of peace.

After all, wasn't that exactly what Benjiro was doing now? Trying to repair what had been rent asunder? He had not asked permission for this strange adventure. No, he was doing what was necessary to ensure the continuity of the clan, and he had done so in defiance of all his upbringing.

After a time, the bug reemerged from the train control room, moving quickly down the aisle. He was struck again by the way the bug moved, the way it seemed to slip from human to inhuman, masculine to feminine. There was the movement of the hips, the shape of them as it skirted the hand poles. The wide shoulders and narrow waist.

Its hands contorted again.

"Give me your hand."

Ben knew the terms of this strange arrangement. He raised a hand. The bug took his hand in its firm grip, placed a small disk against his wrist. With the other hand, the fingers seemed to trill in the air. The voice followed, staccato, toneless.

"You came alone."

"Yes."

"Did you inform anyone of your communication."

"No."

"Does anyone know where you are."

Ben shook his head. How dare they impugn him with the suggestion that he might renege on his word!

The bug removed the disk and slipped it away into the utility belt. Then it sat down across from him, just on the edge of the seat. Ben wanted to ask who the bug was, but he didn't want to seem a fool. The bug had every advantage. It knew where they were, how to control the train. He assumed it was armed. It could hide the secret of its underlying humanity behind the strange mask. He, on the other hand, was, for the first time in his life, utterly powerless.

Unsure what else to do, he leaned back his head and closed his eyes. He must at all costs appear not to be bothered by his circumstances.

THE TRAIN GROUND to an abrupt halt. Ben opened his eyes. The bug had returned to the front of the train and was coming back to him now. The single door opened. The bug rose and indicated that Ben should precede it. He acquiesced, descending a few inches onto a dusty stretch of concrete. Overhead, the tunnel walls arched towards what may once have been decorative tiling. It was impossible to tell.

He half expected another ascent by rope, but the bug indicated a nearby stairwell. Ben searched for any indication of where they might be, but all the station signs had long since been defaced. They ascended into a streetscape utterly unlike the rendezvous.

They were past the squalor of the riverside. Vast towers of sinecure-funded housing stretched into the sky. Glossy and blue, they were not half bad-looking, built several generations after the mid-twentieth century brick monstrosities they had replaced. Ben tipped his head. Between the tips of the buildings, he could make out patches of sky. He may even have seen a star.

Electric buses thrummed past. Where they stopped, long queues of people descended without fuss or hurry.

"Where is this?"

The bug ignored the question. It gestured at a side street. Ben hesitated but decided against appearing trepidatious. They began to walk. No one paid them any mind.

They moved a few blocks away from the subway station. Ben did not know whether they were still in Queensborough, or whether they had made their way into Breuckelen. He felt a tap on his shoulder. The bug indicated a narrow alley between two of the public housing buildings. Ben passed without question into the darkness of the space.

"Turn around."

"Why?"

"For your blindfold."

"What?" For the first time, he felt he may have come up against the limits of his equanimity.

Ben moved as slowly as he dared. So much for protestation. With a practiced motion, the bug cinched a dark band of cloth over his eyes. Then, with an almost tender touch, it took his hand between thumb and two fingers and led him towards their destination.

They passed first through a doorway. Ben was struck by the cacophony of smells, surprised by their richness, their familiarity: cardamom, cinnamon, ginger, chilies. What had he imagined they ate in the outerboroughs? Garbage? *Meat*? His ignorance rankled.

"Elevator."

There was a slight give to the floor as they stepped inside. The doors shut and Ben's stomach dropped. This was not the imperceptible movement he knew from life in Manahatta. He felt a sense of acute precarity.

After a few seconds, the bug directed him through the door, then turned him several times in a circle. The movement was playful, dancelike. They walked a few paces more, then stopped. There was the sound of a knock on a door, no pattern or code that Ben could discern. The door opened, and they passed into another space, again demarcated by smell, which was bold and lively and utterly foreign to him. He was sure at first that he hated it.

They moved across a wooden floor; he knew the sound of his shoes on wood. The bug instructed him to sit. Ben found himself sinking into a cushion, the fabric thick, chunky. His elbows rested on wooden armrests.

"Can I remove the blindfold?"
There was no answer. Ben lifted the cloth from one eye. He was alone.

two

H E WAS NOT sure what he had been expecting. This was not it.

Ben was seated in a living room. The room was dark and cramped to his sensibilities, the kind of space he might have had in the back closets of his Haarlem apartment during graduate studies at Columbia. Across from him was a low green couch and another chair. The rug was Turkish or Afghan, well-worn. The walls were hung with tapestries and chintzy art, no sign of an embedded flatscreen or touchpad. In fact, the entire space was in a surreal analog bubble. This strange fact was driven home by the phantom tremor of his confiscated phone. His fingers dipped into his breast pocket before he caught himself.

Just past the couch was a strip of kitchen. A stainless-steel refrigerator, a meter of countertop space over drawers, and then a stove. Sink in the corner. Past this was a hallway, through which, by craning his neck, he could make out a couple of doors.

In the space that remained was a table, enormous, wooden, and round.

Ben sat for a minute without moving. He could make out no ambient noise from within the apartment. There was noise—laughing, a playful shout—from beyond the front door. He wondered where the bug had gone, whether it still had his phone.

He assumed he was being subjected to some kind of test. Of what, he could not fathom. He had already lived up to his end of the strange deal. Under ordinary circumstances, he'd never acquiesce to such byzantine layers of control and mystery. But if these hoops were necessary to maintain the absolute confidentiality he required, it was worth a few hours of discomfort.

One of the inner doors opened. Ben straightened in his chair. He waited until the figure came into the kitchen before turning his head. Best not to look too eager.

A Black woman in a red-and-yellow dashiki passed through the doorway. She looked him up and down, smiled politely, and greeted him in a language he did not understand. She began to move around the kitchen. The space filled with the rich scent of hot oil, onions, garlic, plantains, and curry.

Ben watched her work. Some kind of maid or servant, by the look of her. She wore cheap blue rubber flip flops and a plastic watch on her left wrist. It was hard to tell how old she was. Older than Ben; perhaps thirty-five or forty. She was plump and pretty, her hair natural and short. She sang to herself under her breath.

There was a sudden rattle at the front door, and Ben turned with a jerk. A lanky Black man came through the door. He too was dressed in bright patterned yellow, with olive trousers and leather sandals. He nodded once to Ben, a slight register of surprise in his eyes, then went to stand by the woman in the kitchen. They spoke in low tones. Ben could make out none of it; he longed for his natural language translator. After a minute, the man took a wooden spoon from the counter and stole a taste of whatever was simmering in the pot. The woman scolded him, and he laughed. He elbowed her playfully on the back and went quickly into one of the back rooms.

Ben wondered how much of this was a performance for him. He did not know the person he had come to meet. He—she? they?—was a digital phantom, known only by a handle, and by reputation. Would he meet the man himself? Was this woman his spy?

Now at last someone came to greet him. Another woman emerged from the hallway by the kitchen. She wore dark jeans and a black shirt patterned with ornate golden silhouettes of flowers. Her eyes were dark, her hijab black. She came through the kitchen, laying a tender hand on the cook's shoulder as she passed through. The cook said something over her shoulder.

The woman came into the living room. "Mr. Nakamura."

Ben rose quickly to his feet. "Yes."

"I am so sorry to keep you waiting. My name is Kiral."

"Are you...M3rlyn?" It was a little silly to use the handle aloud.

Kiral shook her head. "No. Only a liaison. Please, have a seat."

Ben sat again. Kiral took a seat on the couch. A moment later, the cook came over, bearing a tray with a traditional long-stemmed copper Turkish coffee pot and two small copper cups, which she set on the low wooden coffee table between them.

"Thank you, Amina." To Ben: "Have you ever had

Turkish coffee? It's brewed quite strong. We've taken the liberty of pouring it over sugar."

Ben gave a curt nod. He could not recall the last time he had consumed processed sugar. Kiral took the coffee pot by its long handle, poured the coffee into the cups, and set one before him. There was a tiny spoon with the cup. He gave the coffee a stir, then politely took a sip. It was scalding hot, sweet, robust as a mouthful of black soil. It recalled Sunday evenings with his grandmother, whose Syrian coffee, flavored with cardamom, was not so different. Ben eyed Kiral over his cup. Was this the kind of thing they would already know?

He sipped again. Delicious.

"Let's get down to business. We know who you are, sir, and for that reason we were willing to bend the usual protocols. We concur that it is safest to discuss your situation in person, where we can be assured of the privacy of our conversation, without fear of being intercepted by police or security, however well-intentioned." She smiled at this. What Ben was asking her to do was illegal, and they were putting themselves at enormous risk to take him on as a client. "We might not ordinarily have brought a prospective client to our doorstep, but here you are. Let us hear your case from the horse's mouth, so to speak."

Kiral had a lovely, smooth voice, only slightly accented.

Ben sat for a moment. He scanned the room. This was a moment of supreme vulnerability. All the minor humiliations he had endured until now had been in service of maintaining a secret. To reveal that secret was another act altogether, an act of humility, even humiliation, for which no amount of time or worry had prepared him. The stakes of the revelation themselves felt almost fatalistic, as if in merely saying the word aloud, he would be plunged onto an inexorable path forked towards opposing outcomes: either the restoration of peace and prosperity, not just in his own heart, but among the elite families—or eternal shame and humiliation, and the total collapse of his clan.

Dare he reveal such a thing over Turkish coffee in a living room in Queensborough?

He chose his words carefully.

"Many generations ago, after the formal establishment of the cybersinecures, the great families arrogated to themselves artifacts of incalculable worth as symbols of their right to rule. Clan Nakamura, descended as we are of Imperial Japanese Samurai, bears a katana of medieval provenance, a symbol of our status as first among the great clans. The sword, wielded by my family, passed down from generation to generation, was forged by none other than Matsukata."

Kiral smiled politely. Ben rankled. For a moment, he felt he would burst, but he forced his voice to maintain its simmer.

"Matsukata is, inarguably, the finest sword-smith of all time, and the blade is—" Ben stopped himself. None of this mattered. Kiral's interest—her principal's interest—was purely commercial.

Without the sword, he would not be allowed to enter the convocation of the clans and would go unrecognized by his peers. Clan Nakamura would die with his father, and everything they had built up over generations—the land, the tech, the government infrastructure—would be divvied up like so much carrion among vultures.

"Matsukata's blade has been stolen from my family. And I want you to steal it back."

Kiral heard all of this with the same neutral expression. She took another sip of her coffee.

The politeness of his hostess was almost more than he could bear. He tried to regain his equilibrium: had he imagined she would share in his outrage? Fling her coffee down and make a vow to justice? He had to admit that her placidity was working—he had no idea what she was thinking.

"Mr. Nakamura, how do you know that it was not us who stole the Nakamura Matsukata from you?"

Ben twitched. So, she did know the sword. He must assume, too, that she knew its import. A bitter pill to swallow.

"It was inartfully done." His voice was a low growl. "Unless your reputation is nothing more than so much posturing."

Kiral was curt. "I daresay not. We know who stole the sword."

Ben's heart leapt. "I would be curious to know."

"Does it matter? He was only the means, and now that he has his money, I very much doubt he's remained on the continent. The question for you, Mr. Nakamura, is who would want to steal your sword?"

"Nakamura Matsukata is an historical artifact. Many collectors would make great sacrifices for such a prize."

"Any collector of means would occupy, if I may be so blunt, your social stratum, Mr. Nakamura. They've got priceless blades of their own. No, far more importantly, they would understand your rituals and your conventions, as well as the consequences to upending them. The convocation of the clans is in three weeks, and you are expected to attend for the first time as the scion of your family's sinecure. To steal the sword would clearly mean a profound vote of no confidence in your right to rule. We know as well as you that this was no ordinary theft—it was a provocation."

Ben forced himself not to flinch.

"I dare say I am not telling you anything you don't already know. Let me ask you another way: who among your peers would rate you an enemy?"

Benjiro Ibn Benjiro Ayad Nakamura bent his face in great shame. He had hoped not to utter the name, the bitter name, aloud.

"Ernesto Villaseñor."

He could not tell whether the name meant anything to Kiral. Ben collected himself. There was small solace in her professionalism.

"Have you finished your coffee?"

Ben had forgotten all about the coffee. He took another sip or two. It was cold now. "What's next? How do we get this started?"

Kiral nodded absent-mindedly. "Amina?"

The cook came back into the living room. The women spoke for a minute while Amina gathered up the coffee things and retreated again to the kitchen.

Ben frowned. This had gone on long enough.

"I have good news for you, Mr. Nakamura."

"Yes," he said, far more glumly than he'd wished to let on.

"She says she has made enough food for you to join us for supper."

"Supper? I—I...supper! But what about the sword?"

Kiral and Amina looked at him, heads cocked. Their faces bore matching expressions of bemusement.

"Mr. Nakamura." It was Amina who spoke this time. She had a low, rolling voice, more heavily accented than Kiral's. "Do please join us for supper. How else are we supposed to negotiate?"

three

The women—Kiral and Amina—refused to speak of business during the meal. The man, whose name was Mobo, had re-emerged as Amina laid the place settings. He appeared only slightly surprised to find Benjiro still there. He half-cocked an eyebrow, then proceeded to putter around the kitchen with a bottle of beer dangling from his fingertips, studiously avoiding eye contact.

Ben tried once or twice to raise the topic of their negotiations, but each time Kiral deftly turned the conversation away. Ben gave up. Little as he cared for his current circumstances, he was not about to shortchange his prospects by committing an avoidable faux pas.

As for the food, it was unlike anything he had ever had. Each dish was laid out on white porcelain in the center of the table. To his relief, he found that all of it was vegetarian.

"I hope it is not rude to ask," he said, after a few minutes of polite silence, during which everyone served themselves. He had tried a bite of a small fried yellow ball whose taste he could not pinpoint. It was delicious. "What do you call this food?"

"It's good, no?" Mobo grinned. He rose and went to the refrigerator, returning with another beer. "You want one?"

Ben shook his head.

Mobo shrugged and sank heavily into his seat.

"These balls—this is garri. Fermented cassava tubers." Mobo went around the table, indicating each dish with the butt-end of the bottle. "This is some egusi soup, some jollof rice. Ega aganyin; beans. Be careful, my sister makes it hot."

"Your sister?"

Amina nodded. Ben took them both in. He could see it. They had the same cheekbones under distinctive eyes. He guessed that Mobo was older. His beard was greying.

"What kind of food is it?"

Mobo turned to his sister, as if for permission. She only raised an eyebrow.

"Nigerian."

Amina indicated Kiral. "My mother taught us to cook in a refugee camp in the Neue-Netherlands."

Ben had no sense of how to respond to this. He was, frankly, shocked to know this much about them, given who they were, what he was asking of them. "I see."

Ben ate the rest of the meal in silence. Amina and Kiral chatted with one another in Dutch, not, he gathered, about anything of much importance. Mobo finished his meal, leaned back in his chair and took a long slug of beer.

"Sis. Did you make dessert?"

"Yes, but only three portions," Amina said. "And we have a guest. You'll have to go without."

"Ah!" He swatted at her as she rose to grab it from the refrigerator.

She produced a platter of pale brown balls dusted in sugar. They smelled of coconut.

"Shuku shuku, Mr. Nakamura," Amina said, placing the tray before him. "Heavenly."

Ben took one. She was not wrong.

When they had eaten their fill, the hosts worked quickly to clear the table. Between them, the dishes were done, leftover food stored, and a kettle set for tea.

Ben watched them work, fascinated. He had never seen this kind of work firsthand, save for the handful of times servants cleaned up a mess when he and his sisters were children. He could not imagine living like this, having to cook and clean for oneself. And yet the women chatted contentedly as they worked and were soon done.

At some point Mobo finished his beer and left.

When the work was done, Amina gave Ben a cup of scalding hot fragrant tea—rooibos, pungent and bitter. He knew it well, had acquired the taste on safari in Kenya many years ago. She went to sit beside Kiral at the far side of the table.

To his surprise, it was Kiral who spoke. "Mr. Nakamura, if we are to enter into an agreement with you, there are certain conditions that we require to be met. They are, I hope you understand, non-negotiable."

Ben was not sure where he stood. He tried to make a joke. "I had believed this to be a negotiation."

Kiral and Amina exchanged a look.

"This is not the usual remit of our work, Mr. Nakamura. We are taking on more than the usual risk."

What she did not say was that he really had no choice.

Negotiation was a pretext, a euphemism. They had what he needed, and everyone at the table knew it.

"We would like you to remain here with us while we recover the blade."

"But I have—I—"

"It is non-negotiable."

"Can I send word to my staff? My family?"

Kiral shook her head. "Our affairs are conducted in a carefully controlled bubble, Mr. Nakamura. We cannot risk a puncture. You will be missed for a week, perhaps two, but you will be returned intact."

Ben wondered what his family would make of such an absence. A few days might be overlooked as a late Rumschpringe, a chance to cool his nerves before the ascension. Two weeks? His father would be occupied with winding down his administration. He might be needled by Ben's absence, but Ben doubted any annoyance could outweigh his relief. His sisters would be God knows where.

Ben missed none of them.

As for his retinue, the only one who might care was Naomi, his chargé d'affairs. She was discrete, intelligent. If not quite a confidant—in his position, it was unwise to unburden to anyone—he nevertheless trusted her.

Ben ran through the likely course of events. Someone would try to go through his web archives, piecing together clues to his whereabouts. But he had communicated with M3rlyn through the dark web, and he had scrupulously covered his tracks. This was an endeavor he had taken on in perfect secrecy. He did not know how long it would be before they came looking for him. He did not know that he could be found.

He could accept either the terms or the loss of the sword.

He nodded once. "I agree."

Amina placed a hand on Kiral's. She took a sip of tea, set down the cup, and looked Benjiro right in the eyes.

"Then, of course, there is the matter of the price."

He saw now the trap that he had allowed himself to walk into. Acquiescing to their demand to meet in Queensborough. Relinquishing his watch and phone. He still had no idea where they were, for the bug—if indeed it were not one of them—had not reappeared.

Then there was the elaborate home-cooked meal, the rituals of the guest-host relationship. The careful drip-drip of personal details meant, he was sure, to soften him to the tenuousness of their situation.

Even if he ran from the apartment at this moment, he had no way of finding his way back to Manahatta. No money to pay for transportation over the infected river. He might avail himself of a public services office, but he was not willing to debase himself so thoroughly yet.

"The price."

They had him over the coals, now. It was pure economics—the inelasticity of supply, inelasticity of demand. The schedules formed a vertex of right angles. Now, there was only the transfer of wealth, pure and simple.

Amina named her figure.

Ben burst out laughing. It was much more than he had expected. It was extraction, exploitation, monopoly…he could scarcely comprehend his position.

"Am I quite sure I've heard you?"

"Mr. Nakamura, you reached out to solicit my business. I am only naming my price. If you find it unreasonable, you are welcome to take your request to the open market, where, I will remind you, neither discretion nor results are guaranteed."

Despite himself, he was still laughing. "I don't have much of a choice."

Amina waited for him to sober.

Ben could afford it, of course. But there was no doubt it would hurt. His family had amassed unfathomable wealth, but to access and liquidate a sum like this would prove complicated.

"How in God's name am I to make such a transfer?"

"We will leave the logistics for later. After all, at the moment, you have no way to access your funds."

He was genuinely surprised. "You don't want a down payment? Collateral?"

Amina shrugged.

"Are you a man of honor, Mr. Nakamura?"

He might have simply nodded or grunted an assent. The question was rhetorical—except that something in the way she posed it to him made him wonder whether in fact he was. Was he prepared to pay her if she retrieved the blade?

"I am."

"Then I will do the job."

Amina pushed back her chair and rose. "Thank you for joining us for supper." She bent her head to signal the end of their negotiations. "Kiral can show you to the guest room. I am tired and I need to think."

She had started down the hall when a question of supreme urgency rose up. Ben called after her.

"Wait. If you fail…" Ben mustered his self-respect. "I won't pay you if you fail."

Amina pursed her lips, but she was smiling. It was infuriating.

"If I fail, I'll have no need for your money."

four

It wasn't clear to Benjiro how a person could live like this. The apartment's spare room was smaller than many of his closets. There was a low, stiff bed, a dresser and a bookshelf. Black-and-white lithographs on one of the walls. He found them tacky and unmoving.

He had spent the night, and now most of the day, in the room. He had seen no sign of Kiral, Amina or even Mobo since their negotiation the night before. There were other bedrooms in the hall—two, in fact—but their doors were locked. Ben had tried them.

The apartment clearly functioned as a way station. All day, people came and went, some for a quick meal, cooked from the well-stocked pantry, others to collect a book or a folder from a drawer in the kitchen. He rifled through it during a stretch of boredom, searching for clues. It was full of little nothings, romance novels, rubber bands, and school permissions slips to the Zoo.

"Where is Amina?" Ben asked of everyone he saw, emerging from his room like a hermit reentering a desert village, wild-eyed and wary. "I demand to speak to her!"

The answer was always the same: "How on earth am I supposed to know?"

He felt like a prisoner. The bug, whoever it was, had not returned. Or if they had, Ben had no way of recognizing them without the suit.

He was stiflingly bored, an unfamiliar feeling.

The kitchen and living room were his to use as he wished. The lavatory, too, of course. The bookshelf in his room was stocked with books. Many were on the list of "inadvisable" texts: Hobbes, Rousseau, Locke, Smith, de Tocqueville, Marx, Arendt, Butler, Fukayama. This did not surprise him, but the presumptuousness made him prickly and sour. He could not know whether the books had been put there just for him, an esoteric thumbing of the nose. And if they were, well, then just who did these people think they were? He'd been allowed to dabble in them in college, of course, but that was a strictly controlled learning environment, and his educational chaperone had been upfront about their many flaws. She had smiled indulgently when he'd asked to read them. "They're brilliant, Ben. But outdated."

And that was true. Ben recalled very little of the texts, aside from the naïve sense of discovery with which they were imbued—Hobbes, perhaps, exempted. He supposed the shedding of medieval feudalism must have felt like a kind of liberation. The notion that a liberal democratic-capitalist order could emerge from such a chrysalis and achieve a kind of historical finality bordered, to his sensibilities, on the delusional. But had they known then what was understood now about genetics, human psychology, business administration, computer science, AI—it was from the new sciences that the source of stability in human society had finally emerged.

The cybersinecures had seen to that. Life, he had been assured since the earliest memories in the child development center, was finally pleasant, prosperous, and long.

Mobo was the first to arrive in the evening.

Ben was in the living room. Boredom had driven him into the arms of Sir Francis Bacon's *Novum Organum*. At the sight of his ostensible host, Ben snapped shut the book. But Mobo ignored him. He kicked off his workman's boots in the front hall and went to the fridge. He grabbed a bottle of beer, returned to the living room, and sank into a chair, allowing his long legs to unkink before him. When at last he noticed that Ben was there, he indicated the bottle with a long finger and a raised eyebrow. Ben declined.

"How long is this going to take?"

Mobo took a slug of beer. "It's not my business. You have to ask my sister."

That's right, they were brother and sister. Ben wondered how much he could wring from Mobo.

"Remind me where you're from?"

Mobo took another sip. He rolled his tongue about in his mouth, measuring Ben up. How much to reveal?

"I was born in Nigeria. My sister was born in the Neue-Netherlands."

They were refugees. Amina had said as much. He didn't ask whether they were here legally.

"And Kiral?" It wasn't hard to guess. Ben glanced down, reappraised the provenance of the carpet.

"Ask her." Mobo grinned, finished the beer, and rose from his chair. More theatrics of obstruction.

Just then the front door opened, and someone came briskly through. There was the sound of a bag dropping heavily onto the floor, and a pause while laces were undone, boots slipped off. Mobo cocked his head. When he saw who it was, he wrinkled his lip, pushed himself up from the chair and moved brusquely down the hall.

The new arrival came into the living room. Benjiro was transfixed. Shx wore skintight black jeans and a white crop top under a black leather jacket with bright red fringe. Hxr hair was short, black, mussy curls on top, close-cropped on the sides. The hint of a mustache. Shx took Ben in with bright black eyes. Shx wore the slightest bit of cat's eye mascara. Hxr septum was pierced with a silver ring.

"Where is Amina?"

Shx did not seem to hear him. Or perhaps shx did not understand. Shx smiled, pointed to the kitchen, and then bunched hxr fingers and put them to hxr mouth, eyebrow raised inquisitively, as if to say, have you eaten?

In fact, Ben had barely eaten since the night before. Back in Manahatta, Ben's diet consisted of a finely curated series of micro-meals, prepared by his personal chef and consumed at optimized intervals. He had never learned to cook. As such, having been left to fend for himself in the kitchen, he'd done little more than pick at a few things—an apple or two, a few handfuls of almonds, and a panful of scorched nameless tubers, cooked without oil or butter, left unwashed on the range. He was ravenous and hypoglycemic. Yet his breeding demanded that he remain calm.

He shook his head. Shx understood.

Shx went into the kitchen and began to rummage for knives, bowls, onions, produce. When shx had arranged everything on the counter, shx set to work. There was something familiar in hxr movements, the shift of the shoulders, the shape of hxr legs. Recognition hit him.

"You're the bug!"

Shx did not react. Again, it was as if shx had not heard him.

The picture became clearer. The strange hand motions the bug had made—sign language, run through the suit to produce the artificial voice. Shx was deaf.

Ben went and stood beside hxr. It was a moment before shx noticed him.

"You picked me up," he said loudly, as if that would make a difference. Then, feeling foolish, he did his best to mime his words. "The suit, with the eyes like a bug. That was you."

Shx nodded.

Ben looked hxr over again. Shx was quite tall, her shoulders broad, athletic. Shx had removed the red jacket and he saw that hxr forearms were dark-haired, sinewy with muscle.

"What's your name?" he asked while shx watched his lips.

Then, to his surprise, shx spoke, hxr voice high and fuzzy. Shx signed as she mouthed the words. "My name is Alejandrx." Shx pronounced it *Alehandrequis*.

"Are you Mexican?"

Alejandrx shook hxr head. Again, shx signed as shx spoke aloud. "My country is Honduras. I am here legally if this is what you are asking."

Ben scowled and mumbled something in the negative. He was struck in that moment by the smell of onions simmering in oil. Alejandrx turned away from him to scatter a handful of spices into the onions. Ben returned to the living room and pretended to immerse himself in the *Novum Organum*.

Just then there was another perfunctory knock at the door, which opened to reveal another woman. She was a little person, and she was dressed in the uniform of a sinecure sanitation worker—pale green overalls and a forest-green hooded sweatshirt. She bent and removed her boots and hat, emblazoned with the white silhouette of the caduceus, then strode into the kitchen, where she grabbed a beer. She tapped Alejandrx on the elbow and proceeded to speak to her in a stream of Spanish so rapid, Ben felt that she had transcended words and entered a new, higher form of communication. To Ben's surprise, she, too, signed as she spoke. Alejandrx, evidently pleased to see her, replied in sign language alone.

The woman hadn't noticed Ben at first, but when Alejandrx pointed him out with a flicker of her gaze, she turned, pursed her lips, and came over to introduce herself.

"Reina," she said, sticking out her hand. She had lovely dark eyes and silver hair pulled back into a small ponytail.

Ben rose and bowed, but he did not shake.

"It's not contagious," Reina said with a click of her tongue.

Ben cocked his head. "I'm sorry?"

Alejandrx, who had been watching them from the kitchen, snapped several times for Reina's attention. Shx signed something to Reina, who turned back to Ben.

"Shx says it's your custom never to shake hands, and that I shouldn't take it personally. So I won't. When you're my size, you get used to ignoring slights, real or otherwise."

"She?"

Ben's gaze turned to Alejandrx. It was not that he cared. He had slept with men and women and was attracted to both. It was more that he was surprised.

"Shx signs her pronouns with an x to privilege hxr pre-Colombian roots, before the Spanish muzzled hxr people with the gender binary."

"Is shx muxe?"

Reina shrugged. "The only category for Alejandrx is Alejeandrx."

Reina sank down onto the couch and cracked the beer. "Where's Mobo?" she said to no one in particular. "Tell him I owe him a beer."

She scanned the label, raised an eyebrow and drank.

Ben could not shake his discomfort at the informality of everything. So much of his life was made up of highly choreographed rituals, and the anticipation of the convocation had only made things worse. He could not imagine simply showing up at a friend's house, without the formal announcements, the admittance by the butler, the prescribed waiting period during which his host dressed for the evening. And to presume to cook in another person's home…

He turned his gaze once more to Alejandrx. Shx was stirring an enormous pot of something whose fragrance he did not recognize, lost in hxr own world, one hand on hxr hip, which moved to the beat of a song that only shx could hear.

Ben turned his attention back to Reina, who was eyeing him with a smirk. Ben scowled. Reina raised her eyebrows in an exaggerated display of innocence and tipped back the beer.

Again, the door opened. This time there was not even a knock. A stooped older man came in. He was dressed in a rumpled overlarge pale grey suit complete with an old-fashioned green necktie. He wore round-rimmed glasses, and his longish hair was swept back away from his face. He was carrying a long black cylindrical case across his back.

"Hong!" Reina shouted from the couch.

Hong gave a start and turned towards the living room, his eyes wide behind his glasses. Reina hopped down from the couch, and ran into the foyer, where he knelt and embraced her.

"Who else is here? Amina?"

"No, you're one of the first. Want a beer?"

Hong made a sour expression. "Let me put this somewhere."

He pulled the cylinder from behind his back—Ben wondered for a moment whether it contained a sword, asinine as the thought may have been—and set it down in the umbrella stand just inside the door.

He was turning to close the door when another person came lumbering through, almost knocking him over.

"Hong!" It was less a voice than a peal of thunder. The man, so tall he had to stoop to make it through the doorframe, took Hong's hand and shook vigorously. Hong practically flailed in the man's great mitt.

Only then did the new man fully unfurl himself. He was simply enormous, tall and broad-chested. He had a bushy grey walrus mustache and wild grey hair. His eyes were small, deeply creased with laugh lines. He wore a long black coat over work pants and heavy boots.

"Queenie!" The furniture rumbled with his voice.

"Dmitri, my darling," Reina replied. Dmitri came slowly down onto one knee so that they could embrace. His coat billowed with the movement like a sail before Boreas, and Reina for a moment was engulfed by it.

"I'd carry you in, but I threw out my god-damned back," Dmitri scowled. "Here, Hong, give me a shove, help these old knees to unbend once and for all."

He set a hand for half a moment on Hong's case, thought better of it at the sound of Hong's gasp, and used the wall to steady himself as he rose once more to his great height. He slipped off his vast coat and draped it carelessly over the coatrack..

"I'm ravenous. Who's cooking? Amina? Your breath smells like beer, my queen. I'll take half a dozen if that slow bastard, Mobo, won't miss 'em. Who's this?"

He had noticed Ben. He came into the living room.

"A new fellow, eh? I never saw the job description."

"That's the client," Reina explained.

"Prospective client," Hong corrected.

There was a sound from the kitchen. Dmitri went there next. Alejandrx saw him out of the corner of hxr eye and gave him a finger wave. Dmitri, like Reina, signed to hxr as he spoke. "The Maid of Aragon!

Forgive me for not seeing you before."

Alejandrx blew him a kiss.

"Whatever the hell you're making, double it. Triple it! I could eat a bear. And I just might."

Everyone laughed as if he had said something uproarious.

Ben found that he was standing. His instincts told him that he should be ready to bow to the new arrivals, yet neither had yet come forward to introduce himself. He had no idea what he was expected to do in these circumstances. He thought that he might retreat to his room.

The big man turned to him from across the room. He must have been almost seven feet tall. "Dmitri Madrid," he said, by way of introduction. "You've met the others."

"Not yet," Hong came tentatively forward. He bowed from the waist. "Hong Piao. Please call me Patrick."

"My name is Benjiro Ibn Ben—"

"Good to meet you, Benjie," Dmitri flashed him a strange sign, his fist bunched, his thumb erect. "Queenie, you're holding out on me."

He went to the fridge and drew from it half a six pack, which dangled by a loop from his thumb. While he raided, Hong and Reina came into the living room to sit. They had just sunk down onto the couch, talking about a restaurant in a neighborhood Ben had never heard of, when the front door opened yet again.

Ben shook his head. He felt he was in some kind of carnival side show. If this was the team that Amina had assembled for his purposes, he may have been conned. His mouth tightened. He did not like to be manipulated. If this was a con, an exploitation, a ransom, there would be bloody retribution.

To his great relief, Kiral and Amina came through the door. They took a minute to remove their shoes and pull on house slippers.

Kiral wore a pale blue kaftan, with delicate gold floral embroidery around the collar and wrists.

Her hijab was yellow. Her eyes shone. Amina was dressed more casually, in dark jeans, white blouse, and a red waist-length jacket. Her ears were hung with big gold hoops, and she carried a large brown paper sack.

Amina acknowledged him with a nod, but she went to the kitchen to chat with Alejandrx. She drew from the paper sack several bottles of wine, which she set on a wooden rack. Kiral came into the living room to greet Ben. Her manner was familiar, if a little stiff.

"Mr. Nakamura. I trust that you have been comfortable."

He didn't have time to answer.

"It's ready," Amina called to her. She and Alejandrx had begun to pull stacks of plates from cupboards, piles of silverware from drawers. The others—Hong, Reina, Dmitri—rallied, and began to assist in setting the table.

"Wonderful," Kiral smiled warmly. "We'll eat together, Mr. Nakamura."

"I am tired of all the meals." Ben tried to keep his voice level. Tired of the stalling, rather. His stomach growled. "What about a plan?"

Ben saw that all of them had stopped to await Kiral's answer. Even Mobo had reemerged from the hallway. He stood between Amina and Dmitri, a half-smile on his lips, wondering, too, at the mysterious verdict.

It was Amina who responded to him.

"I don't know about you, Mr. Nakamura, but I cannot plan on an empty stomach."

FIVE

BEN SAT DOWN, chastened. Amina had put him in his place, yet she had done so with tact and grace.

In fact, he was surprised by how little of the moment lingered. Among his peers, manners prevented anyone from dwelling on unpleasant outbursts, but from childhood he had been unconsciously schooled in the subtle art of exchanged glances, raised eyebrows, averted looks—the petty, cloying way that his class reinforced the prescriptions of one another's behavior.

At the table, now, there was none of that. His brief outburst was already forgotten.

The food, once again, was delicious. There were black beans, rice, a pungent, spicy tomato and onion salsa, and small dumplings of lightly fried cornmeal dough, stuffed with something that Benjiro could not quite put his finger on. There was maize, drizzled in spicy honey, and the wine that Amina had brought. Ben had sipped it with some misgiving and was forced, again, to concede that it was quite fine.

As he ate, Ben took in the motley crew. With Amina and Kiral he was now somewhat familiar. Mobo, too, though of course the man had denied any association with his sister's operation. Of the dinner guests, he was the least engaged, his attention mostly on the food and the endless stream of beers he pulled from the fridge.

Dmitri Madrid was almost too much to take in all at once. He sat in his chair as if squatting on it. The silverware was a toy in his hands. A glass of wine sat untouched beside his plate. He guzzled beers from the can and told raucous stories that Ben couldn't follow, but which made the others laugh. No one was as amused by these stories as he, and more than once he went so far as to clap Ben hard on the back when his own laughter became too much to bear.

To Ben's left was Reina. She mostly ignored him; Dmitri held her rapt. Ben saw that sometimes when he spoke, she mouthed the words in silent echo. He wondered whether he had broached some unspoken seating arrangement, in coming between them. Wondered, too, whether Dmitri saw in her gaze what he did.

There was no head to the table, but Kiral and Amina were at its poles. Beside Kiral sat Patrick Hong, and beside Amina, her brother. When he was not listening to Dmitri, he and Amina spoke in low voices in their mother tongue. Mobo was the more animated, but their conversation was convivial. Fraternal.

Ben and his sisters shared their lineage, their schooling, and their access to the estates. Little else. Most of the time, they saw next to nothing of one another. On the rare occasions they were all together in Manahatta—Sakura lived most of the time in Paris with her husband, Sumaya in Cambridge for her graduate studies—it was usually in preparation for a convocation of the clans. They were brushing up on protocol, not swapping war stories from childhood misadventures.

To watch Amina and Mobo, to see the easy pleasure they took in one another's company, filled Ben with a sense of something new and unfamiliar. It might have been envy, except that these people could have nothing he envied.

Having surveyed these others, Ben turned his attention at last to Alejandrx. His stomach fluttered, and he had the strange sensation that he had been savoring this moment.

This person before him, all contradictions—dark-haired, bright-eyed, gentle and powerful, warm and aloof—he wanted hxr with a fierceness that made him feel that he was going mad.

Shx glanced his way, as if halfway through a thought, and in meeting his eyes lost it. Neither blinked. All around them, the others ate and drank and laughed, somehow unaware that in that room, the very air itself had come alive.

When the meal was over, they rose in concert and began to clear the table. Ben sat, for he was used to having his place cleared. Alejandrx reached across the table for his plate. It was not until shx was almost at the sink that Ben realized his mistake. Several times as a young man he had read Plutarch's *Lives* and had been struck particularly by the life of Alcibiades, a man of noble birth who strove to be greatest in his circumstances. When in Athens, he lived an unapologetic life of decadence and luxury. When, however, he went to war, there was no man better suited to the roughness of the elements.

Ben strove always to emulate this temperament. Here he was among the people of the outerboroughs, with all of their strange customs. He was meant to have cleared his own spot and to assist in the cleaning up. He flushed to realize how inattentive he had been to his own internal code.

He rose quickly and went to the sink, where shx stood rinsing the dishes before setting them in the dishwasher. He stood lamely beside her until shx noticed him, and, smiling, took pity on him. Shx handed him a freshly rinsed plate, and he turned and set it alongside the others in the dishwasher. They did this a couple of time, Alejandrx rinsing, Ben transferring the plates from the stream of water in the sink to the dishwasher.

After a minute, shx burst out laughing, a strange, guttural sound. Shx stifled it with the back of her hand, then steadied hxrself.

"Coffee!" Kiral set a tray down at the center of the round table. Again, there was the set of copper Turkish coffee accoutrements, a little battered around the edges, but the engravings were as exquisite as anything his grandmother had owned.

Mobo, who had been standing off to the side with Dmitri, an open bottle of whisky on the counter between them, made as if to head back down the hall to his room. His sister put a hand on his elbow as he passed.

"Perhaps we will need you, too, this time."

His surprise was evident. The corners of his mouth turned down. He scanned the others' faces as they resumed their places at the table, but his eyes lingered on Benjiro. For a long time, he seemed to be working it out for himself. His eyes flickered to Alejandrx, then Hong, Reina and finally, Kiral. He nodded once in assent. Then he poured himself another two fingers of liquor and sidled to the table.

Ben returned to his own seat and poured himself a coffee from the press. Alejandrx, across from him, sipped Turkish coffee. There was a minute of rattling cups and saucers, cream passed in a ring around the table. Dmitri rose to top off his drink.

When at last everyone had settled, Amina and Kiral exchanged a significant look. Kiral bent her head and Amina nodded. It was she who spoke.

"Mr. Nakamura, you have now broken bread with M3rlyn. We have agreed to terms, and so we will dispense with all formality. Until our duty to you is done, you are one of us. The rest of us have come to know one another over many years. There is deep trust here. We offer that same trust to you. Do you accept it?"

All eyes were on him. The expressions that took him in were curious, patient.

"Yes."

"When we are seated at this table, there is but one rule. Speak your mind honestly or do not speak at all. There may be dissent, but you will know where each of us stands. We expect the same of you. Do you accept this?"

"Yes."

Then, to Ben's surprise, Reina put her hand on his. Gave it a little squeeze.

Alejandrx watched him, observant. He could not know what shx was thinking.

"Mobo, do you, too, agree?"

Again, Mobo's face registered surprise. He too assented.

"Hear, hear," Dmitri said, raising his glass. Mobo grinned. Ben thought his eyes rather mirthless.

"My brother, Mr. Nakamura, is an electrician by trade. I believe we may have need of his expertise."

"Mr. Hong," here the man raised his hand, "is an archivist and librarian.

"Ms. Öztürk, whom you know, is our consigliere."

Kiral blushed and laughed. She shook her head and spoke for herself. "I'm a bank teller, Mr. Nakamura."

Amina indicated with a gesture that they should continue around the table. Reina was next. "Ms. Acevedo?"

"Deputy chief of operations for the sanitation department. Retired."

Ben nodded. They skipped him.

"I'm a magician," Dmitri Madrid said with a wink.

Amina was smiling. "Mr. Madrid is a mechanical engineer."

Dmitri drained his glass. "True enough, I suppose."

The circle had returned to Amina. "As for me, I am a cook and housekeeper. And now, Mr. Nakamura, why don't you take a moment to introduce yourself?"

It was not lost on him that they had skipped Alejandrx.

He stared at hxr across the table. He had noticed, of course, that when they were around the table, they addressed one another formally. "What about you? What is your surname?"

There was a tremor in the air around the table. He did not know whether they had expected him not to notice. That shx had not yet answered suggested that there was something there to know.

Shx signed hxr answer. Reina spoke hxr words aloud: "My surname is del Lago."

"And what do you do?"

Alejandrx met his gaze. For a long time shx did not answer. No one elected to speak in hxr stead.

At last, shx made another flickering sign.

This time it was Amina who spoke for her.

"Alejandrx is my ninja."

six

HE ALMOST SNORTED in response. There hadn't been ninja since…he was being obtuse. Just a day ago, shx had extracted him, brought him here, all as effortlessly as—as a breeze picks up a leaf.

He understood from their collective silence that he could defer no longer. He turned his eyes to Amina, a small gesture of acknowledgement that he had broached once again their balance of expectations.

"My name is Benjiro Nakamura. I am the…but surely you know."

There was a murmur of assent from around the table. He avoided Alejandrx's eyes.

"For fifty generations, my family have been stewards of the Nakamura Matsukata. The blade has been stolen from us. Without it, I cannot enter the convocation of the clans to assume my rightful place as Scion of Clan Nakamura.

"Ms.… " He did not know how to address Amina. "I'm afraid I do not know your surname."

"Adeyemi," her brother responded. "Our surname is Adeyemi."

Amina nodded.

"I have asked Ms. Adeyemi to help me recover the sword. She has agreed."

"Thank you, Mr. Nakamura. As I'm sure you've gathered, M3rlyn is a collective endeavor. Sometimes there are more of us, sometimes fewer. Everyone you see here tonight was invited to participate because they have a skill necessary to recover the sword."

"Does that mean you know where it is?"

The question took Amina by surprise.

Ben continued. "If you didn't have some sense of what it would take, why invite this particular set of people?"

Amina raised an eyebrow and gave Kiral a significant look.

"Well-observed, Mr. Nakamura."

Ben glanced across at Alejandrx. What did he want from hxr? Approval for his deduction? He turned his gaze quickly away.

"That's not all." He found the words coming quickly. "In the spirit of complete honesty."

"Yes?"

"What do you need me for?"

"Why would we—" it was Reina who spoke, but Amina raised her hand and her voice trailed off.

"You're sharper than we expected. As it happens, it took very little to ascertain the whereabouts of the sword."

"Really? Who has it?" Ben's heart was pounding.

Kiral this time: "It was precisely whom you suspected."

Villaseñor, the bastard. Ben wondered what his endgame was. His infrastructure wasn't robust enough to integrate Nakamura-sinecure. Unless his family's spies were much mistaken.

No, Ben very much doubted this. It was something else, something more personal.

Ben and Villaseñor had spent the better part of a decade in a not-quite-friendly rivalry, each of them testing the boundaries of the other's state security apparatus, not so much to make a real break-in as to showcase their respective talents for code breaking. Until the theft of the sword, Ben could not have imagined Villaseñor threatening the balance of power between the cybersinecures.

As a result of this rivalry, which consisted primarily of bragging rights among the elite circle of hackers with whom they communicated on the dark web, Ben had developed a feel for Villaseñor's style, his quirks, the same way a chess grandmaster's repeated matches against a rival reveal might profound insights into their style of play.

Clearly, Villaseñor had done the same. The picture was starting to become clear. Ben himself had written vast swathes of the security code that protected the blade in its vault. Villaseñor, it appeared, had breached the code, and now, he had set Ben a puzzle: steal back the sword, or fail to ascend at the convocation. If Ben succeeded, it would all be chalked up to a bit of friendly rivalry. If Ben failed, he little doubted Villaseñor would move in for the kill. The Nakamura sinecure would be dissolved, its pieces meted out among the remaining clans.

All this ran through Ben's mind in a moment.

"You knew all of this before I contacted you."

Amina nodded. "Word travels quickly in our circles."

"Do you know where the sword is?"

"Not precisely."

"But you need me."

Amina cocked her head.

"You need me close. Otherwise, why bother to keep me around at all? Why not recover the sword, return it for the bounty"—he could not resist the jab—"and be done with it? You know how he's secured it, and you need me to break the code."

That was it. It was obvious now. Ernesto Villaseñor was among his only rivals, and if this was a taunt, he would anticipate that Benjiro would come after the sword himself. Which meant that there would be a digital lock. Ben may have written the Nakamura Matsukata's security code himself, but he had not written it with an eye towards perfect impermeability, because its theft had been unimaginable. It irked him that the code had apparently been so easy to break, but it was clear that Amina suspected Villaseñor would not be so blasé.

There was a strange tension around the table.

Ben did not know whether he had broken some unspoken rule, or whether he had simply come too close to the truth too soon. Either way, he did not care. He knew now what he wanted from all of this.

"I have one more condition. Non-negotiable, to borrow the phrase."

All eyes were locked on him. He set his gaze on Amina.

"I want to be the one to retrieve the sword."

SEVEN

For a long time, the others were silent.

In the end, it was Reina, not Amina, who spoke.

"Mr. Nakamura, we use the planning session to dictate our roles. Not the other way around."

"That would be inefficient," Hong added. He, more than any of the others, was distressed by the strange turn of events, and had begun to rock back and forth. Alejandrx took Hong's hand, which comforted him.

Ben awaited their response.

It irked him that they had not already acquiesced. It was an unfamiliar feeling. Ben stiffened in his resolve. "Nevertheless. I am the client. I must insist. *I* will retrieve the sword."

Dmitri Madrid put a hand on Ben's shoulder. "I think you misunderstand the nature of power." He gave a gentle squeeze. There was a smile buried beneath his mustache.

"Do I?"

"Where is the power at this table?" It was Alejandrx now, spoken aloud in her strained voice.

Ben bristled. "All power flows from authority."

"And who here has authority?"

"I do."

"What authority?"

"The job is mine, the money mine. I am scion of clan Nakamura, hereditary leader of the cybersinecure."

"Not without the sword."

Alejandrx tilted hxr head, widened hxr eyes. Shx sat back in hxr seat.

Ben was silent.

"We do not have to do the work. You cannot make us. We have chosen, each of us, to engage in this venture." Reina spoke for hxr, and it took a moment for Ben to realize that it was because she was translating from Spanish.

"You say the power flows from you, and your authority." Alejandrx went on. "Yet that authority is a potentiality. Without us, you are just another man with hereditary wealth. Your claims to authority rest on the symbolic value of an old piece of metal. Yet that symbol is all too real, for you would not be here in this room were it not for the fact that your peers have agreed to recognize you as one of them only if you're holding that piece of metal when you ask them to recognize the power that you claim to be yours by right. Who holds the power then?"

Ben's lip curled, but he was silent. He knew that if he opened his mouth again, he would only look more a fool to these ideologues. However wrong they might be, they were sharp-witted and articulate to a person.

Shx needn't continue. To hxr credit, shx didn't.

Amina: "We are here to craft a plan for the successful retrieval of the Nakamura Matsukata. I would argue that it is in our mutual interest. We need one another. Who knows; maybe it is possible for you to recover the sword yourself? After all, you are one of us now. Let us design our plan."

Ben was struck again by the shift in tone around the table. Alejandrx, Hong, Reina, Dmitri—they had challenged him, perhaps even bested him, but the charge of the confrontation was gone. It was as if it had never happened. For his part, still bruised, he was determined to speak only when necessary.

"I have confirmed that it was Ernesto Villaseñor who arranged for the theft of the sword."

Ben forgot his resolve immediately. "How? Can you be sure?"

Amina smiled. "I have my methods, Mr. Nakamura. Perhaps one day I will share them with you."

She said something in undertones to her brother, who nodded and rose from the table. Amina indicated Hong.

"I asked Mr. Hong to retrieve the architectural blueprints for each of the Villaseñor estates."

"Oh, yes, of course!" Hong too rose from the table and went to retrieve the architect's case in the umbrella stand.

He and Mobo returned to the table at the same time, Mobo with a collapsible easel, a large pad of white paper and a handful of colored markers. Mobo propped up the easel and affixed the paper to the crossbar. Hong, meanwhile, unscrewed the case and tipped out half a dozen blueprints.

Ben leaned forward. He was perturbed. It had never occurred to him that the estates' plans could be accessed by the public, and by a librarian outside of the sinecure.

"This is the Kykuit…" Ben had been there once or twice, including for Villaseñor's wedding.

"That's right." Hong shuffled through the stack of blueprints, indicating the top left corner of each. "You can—you can see the names there. Easy to read, and there's a legend. This one is, ah, the ranch in Michoacán. The—the, uh, former Presidential Palace in Ciudad de México."

Ben was stuck on the blueprints' provenance.

"I'm sorry—these were in the library?"

"No. No." Hong gave a high, nervous laugh. "Like Ms. Adeyemi, I have my methods. Rather, I should say, contacts."

"Mr. Nakamura, where do you think he'll have stowed the sword?" Kiral indicated to Hong that he should slide the stack over to Ben.

Ben flipped through the documents, trying to let his instincts guide him. He was still unsettled by the open calling out of his powerlessness. He had not been able to meet Alejandrx's eyes.

"Not in México. Transporting it back and forth would be too much effort. Perhaps on the Vineyard?"

He found the mansion on the Vineyard. His gut told him he was straying too far afield. He went back to the top of the stack. There were reasons to recommend any of them.

Ben raised his eyes. The others were awaiting his determination. So, they needed him after all.

"I would guess that it is here. He'll be sure to have the strongest security..."

It made sense intellectually. The Walter Grinnan Robinson House in Nuevo Orlin would be the best-armed of Villaseñor's properties, being the nearest in real terms to the Nakamura cybersinecure's geo-footprint, which ran as far south as Atalanta.

Amina wrote Grinnan Robinson at the top of the pad and next to it a question mark.

Kiral reached for the blueprint, turned it with her fingerprints so that it faced her. She conferred for several minutes with Reina and Hong, who clearly understood best how to read it.

"Can we build it?"

"It would—it would be complex, but yes, the room is perfectly adaptable," Hong responded. "I'll need a day or two to figure out the most efficient order."

"As long as we drill, and they know the breaks won't be there." Reina this time. "But it's no worse than the Prado."

Kiral nodded. She chewed unconsciously at the corner of her lip. "Any intuitions as to where inside? What's this room?"

"Likely to be server storage," Reina said. "Look, you've got ductwork here," She traced a white line across the blueprint, "...with vent shafts connected directly to the HVAC unit here. Which is clever, because they've got—" Reina flipped to another of the sheets, denoting another floor of the old mansion, "cold storage adjacent to the kitchen. It's very tight design. Assuming I'm right."

"Electrically, this makes sense too, for wiring it all together from a box," Mobo chipped in. He had sunk low into his seat, still clasping a beer between his palms, his thumbs drumming philosophically on the open mouth of the bottle.

"Any sense of where he would keep the sword?" Kiral again. "Or anything of value, for that matter."

Reina glanced up at Ben, only half curious as to his response. He shrugged. Villaseñor prized efficiency in his work and in his dominion, at the expense of beauty.

Ben and Ernesto Villaseñor had met many times. Ben was always struck by his lack of personal care. Dark clothes, close-cropped hair, a sparse beard. His glasses were not of the contemporary style. He was thin but soft, almost paunchy.

There was nothing of the carefully cultivated beauty nurtured by the Nakamuras and their people. The hand-stitched clothing, the ornate beadwork, the silhouettes. Ben's clothes fit him like a second skin.

The Nakamura estates, too, were a marvel of aesthetics, drawing equally from the ornate Syrian and Taoist Japanese of his heritage. There was the bonsai greenhouse, the mosaic wood paneling in his study. The grain of the bamboo mats in his sauna had been aligned by hand.

This was as it should be. They were the preeminent clan, and the Nakamura Matsukata symbolized this primacy. It was the most beautiful by far of the familial artifacts, from the carved ebony insert at the base of the tsuka to the gold-flecked thread of the ito.

Ironic, perhaps, that they, more than any of the other clans, were so close to one another in geographic terms, with Nakamura sinecure sprawling westward from the outer boroughs and Manahatta, and Villaseñor's radiating eastward from Ciudad de México. They were the only sinecures on the eastern seaboard.

Except that was not literally true.

Each of the clans kept a consulate in the others' dominions, with the legal stipulation of radical insulation from one another's networks. It was an archaic if effective tradition meant to ensure a sense of mutual vulnerability. Of course, they probed one another's security routinely, but the efforts were meant more as an exercise than a real sortie.

These consulates tended to be clustered nearby to one another in each of the sinecures' densest cities. The consulates on Manahatta consisted of a row of townhouses on a narrow strip of land on the upper east side of the city, directly adjacent to the river.

Matsukata's blade had been stored in the archives of the old Metropolitan Museum.

From there to the Villaseñor consulate was a mere eight blocks.

"Wait."

Again, all eyes were on Benjiro.

"I know where he is keeping the sword."

eight

Mobo woke him early.

"What time is it?"

Mobo glanced at a watch. "Five. Let's go upstairs."

Amina had provided him with an assortment of fresh clothes, straightforward athletic wear. Ben pulled on a hooded jacket

Mobo didn't bother with the pageantry of a blindfold. They rode the elevator to the top floor, then ascended another couple of floors by stair until they arrived at a big steel door. Mobo shoved it open with his shoulder and they stepped out onto the roof.

The view was stunning. They were one in a sea of skyscraper apartments, stretching out in every direction, lit at that hour only by the occasional window. In the distance was the East River, visible now only as a strip of lightless black that ran between the distant lights. Beyond it, Manahatta. For a moment Ben's heart ached.

He heard the sound of a VTOL descending, and he raised a hand to keep the dust from whipping into his eyes. The cab alighted on the rooftop, folded back its blades, and slid open the door.

Ben climbed in. Mobo drew something from his pocket, pointed it towards the VTOL's dash, and stepped away.

Ben was confused. "Aren't you coming?"

"I have a real job." Mobo grinned and stepped away from the closing doors. A moment later Ben was airborne.

Alejandrx was waiting for him in the lot beside the warehouse. Shx was dressed in black leggings and an oversized green hoodie. Hxr hair was wet, slicked back. Ben descended from the cab, and shx indicated with a jerk of hxr head that he should follow.

"Where are we?" he asked, forgetting shx could not hear him.

They entered the warehouse through a side door. The warehouse was at least three stories high, and completely empty, save for a two-story rectangular structure in the corner. On the bottom story there was a door, and Amina emerged from it as they came inside. She waved, then closed and locked the door behind her.

Hong, Reina and Dmitri were in the near corner, removing a tarp from a tall crate-like structure. Dmitri gave the thing a shove but it failed to move. He kicked at its base with one of his great boots, there was a click, and the thing began to roll. It took all of the man's strength to navigate the structure to the center of the warehouse.

Ben and Alejandrx met them there.

It was a curious contraption, steel, square-based,

about two meters wide and twice as tall. Dmitri was sweating from exertion. He mopped his forehead with the cuff of his grey flannel shirt and gave Ben a wink.

"Where's the cord? And the box? Did we forget the box?" There was a note of panic in Hong's voice. He looked a wreck. He was still dressed in his rumbled suit, and the back of his hair was raised in a cowlick.

Reina squeezed his arm. "I've got it. Don't worry. I'm not going to forget the box. Take a few deep breaths."

Hong nodded and drew in three deep breaths. Reina breathed alongside him.

"Better?"

Hong nodded. He cast a quick glance at Ben and turned back to the structure.

Amina handed Reina the keys to the office. "Lock when you come out."

She turned to Ben.

"You must be curious."

He nodded.

"This is the Descartes Room."

"Beg pardon?"

"Here, hand that to me."

Reina had returned from the office with a small white box, from which extended a length of black cord. In the other arm, she carried an extension cord. Hong took the box, while Alejandrx ran the extension cord to an outlet. He plugged the cord into the base of the structure, then drew from his hip pocket a slim leather case.

He pulled a thumb drive from the case and slipped it into a port on the box.

From the far wall, Alejandrx gave a sign.

"Shx says it's ready," Dmitri said.

Hong nodded and flipped open the box to reveal a touchpad. He tapped it a few times, and there was a sudden buzz.

"Step back, lad." Dmitri shooed Ben back.

The base began to extend outwards, moving quickly, not quite silently. As it expanded, Ben saw that what had appeared to be a slatted crate-like case was in fact several dozen beams that stretched from the base to top of the structure. In three seconds, the base had quadrupled its footprint.

The floor of the thing had somehow stretched with it, so that it now constituted a kind of open-air room within the warehouse.

"Go ahead and touch it."

Ben approached, set his fingers gingerly on one of the beams. He knelt. The floor was pliable to the touch.

"Oh, I forgot. Remove your hand." Hong tapped in a command.

The air thrummed with static electricity.

"Touch it again."

Ben reached gingerly for the floor. Hard as steel.

"I don't understand."

"It's a Cartesian machine." Hong was pleased to explain it. "I can convert any blueprint into a set of instructions. Feed them in here," he raised the box, "and the instructions adjust the size of the frame.

"The floor is a micro-folded origami fabric embedded with copper particles that can be fixed with a charge. Oh! Watch."

He tapped the screen again, and two dozen of the vertical beams began to slide into configuration around the base. Ben saw now that they were connected by a series of bright red nylon threads that stretched with their movement, spaced at half-inch intervals.

"Those are the walls."

"It's very clever. But why?"

"We can create any space we wish with it. Do you want to be able to navigate, uh, a bank floor in the dark?" Hong made some adjustments and the room before them expanded into a rectangular shape, the nylon walls reconfiguring to create a series of smaller rooms within the space. "Drill here until you know the space by heart."

"So, we'll practice?"

Hong nodded. "When I get the plans for the consulate, I'll be able to—"

He was running out of the ability to speak.

"We will be able to recreate the consulate here in the warehouse," Amina said. "That way, when we go in, we will already know it."

Ben nodded. "What about furniture?"

"Go ahead, step inside."

Ben tried to step up onto the base but realized he was blocked by a stretch of nylon wall.

"There's a doorway over there," Reina indicated, and he saw that there was a space where the vertical beams were unconnected.

Ben stepped gingerly onto the floor. There was none of its former pliability. If he hadn't seen the machine expand to its current configuration, he'd never have believed it was possible.

Hong tapped out a few instructions and there was a series of blinding flashes. Ben covered his eyes. Somewhere Reina hollered, "Sorry! Should have warned you. It's ok, now."

When he moved his hand, the red threads of nylon appeared to have been drywalled, the room filled with furniture: a desk, comfortable chairs, even a computer monitor on an arched base. The walls were hung with masterworks from history: Rembrandt, van Gogh, Kahlo, Wiley.

Ben was still reeling from the light. "What the hell?"

"Touch it."

He reached for the corner of a nearby desk, expecting to feel the smooth wood of its varnished surface. Instead, his fingers passed into a pool of light, thousands of microbeams crawling up his forearm as he pushed deeper into the hologram.

He burst out laughing. "It's ingenious. How in God's name did you—?"

Dmitri Madrid, who had stepped aside for the demonstration, and was now leaning against the near corner, raised his hand.

"Magic."

"You can step down from there, Mr. Nakamura," Amina said. "It is time to begin your training."

NINE

Hong tapped the pad. In an instant, the illusion was gone. There was a slight electric thrum, and the walls began to shift and reconfigure themselves. Ben hopped quickly down. In another minute the Descartes Room had collapsed into its original shape. Hong unplugged the box, handed it over to Reina with ceremonial flourish.

"I should go." He turned to Amina. "With any luck, I'll have it by tomorrow. I can't promise."

"We will keep ourselves busy. I have my own meetings to keep, today."

Ben watched them leave, careful to keep his expression mild. He was disconcerted that Amina would be gone. It may have been a delusion, but he felt that he understood her. She wanted his money, lots of it. As they had sketched the contours of the plan last night, he had been forced to admit that she seemed to understand its whole.

And her contributions were clever. She had proposed swapping out the Nakamura Matsukata with a perfect replica.

She had said it jokingly, but Ben's mind had run wild with the possibilities of such an idea. If they swapped in a fake, Villaseñor would be none the wiser when he tried to make his move. Ben tried to imagine the look on his face when he revealed that he had, in fact, not only recovered the true sword, but done so in such a way that he could show Villaseñor up before the clans.

"But how do we make a forgery?" Kiral had brought things crashing down to reality. Ben's heart sank. How indeed?

"I could try," Madrid had suggested. "I know a fellow could give me a primer."

"Really?" Amina herself had cocked her head.

Madrid had nodded slowly, tapping out a rhythm on the rim of his empty tumbler as he thought through the details.

"The room is built. What else am I to do?"

Ben hadn't known then what the room was.

"Very well," Amina had agreed. She turned to the easel and wrote: *forge copy of sword?* "I will get you whatever you will need."

Madrid helped to push the Descartes Room back into its corner, then gathered up the extension cord, which he handed off to Reina.

"Don't know when I'll be seeing you, Queenie," he said, kneeling again to embrace her. She kissed each of his cheeks.

Madrid rose on his bad knees and winked at Ben.

"Keep yourself out of trouble, lad. I've got a sword to make."

IN THE SECOND story of the structure in the corner, there was a conference room with a collapsible desk at the center, and a stack of folding chairs in the corner. One of the walls was hung with a whiteboard.

Alejandrx took a chair from the stack and set it before the table. Shx indicated that Ben should sit.

"What are we doing here?"

Shx turned to the whiteboard and began to write. It took a minute, but when shx stepped away, the words were neatly printed.

Monks in Canterbury took a vow of silence.

Shx turned to Ben. He nodded.

There is an 11th century manuscript showing 127 hand signs for aspects of their daily lives.

Again, Ben nodded. An interesting answer. Oblique. Clarifying.

"I see."

Satisfied, Alejandrx drew a capital A. Then shx raised hxr hand in a fist. Shx underlined the A and made the fist again.

Ben too made a fist. Alejandrx shook hxr head. Shx came over to him, took his hand in hxrs and moved his thumb from the knuckles to nestle beside his pointer finger. Shx returned to the whiteboard and drew an S beside the A. Then shx toggled hxr thumb back and forth as shx had done for him. Beside the finger: *A*. Across the knuckles: *S*.

Ben imitated. "I understand."

They proceeded through the alphabet. Alejandrx would draw the letter, and then shx would demonstrate the sign, sometimes making small corrections. Ben learned quickly.

Alejandrx smiled. Shx began to run through the alphabet with hxr hand, slowly at first, so that Ben could keep up, and then faster. After a moment, hxr head began to bop from side to side.

Shx laughed hxr strange laugh. "Like the song."

"Do you know music?"

Hxr expression fell. Shx signed as shx spoke her answer aloud: "I was not always deaf. There are…echoes."

Shx collected hxrself. "Try with the song."

Ben nodded and began to sing. "A, B, C, D, E..."
"Wait! That's not E."

As shx took his hand and moved the fingers up, Reina came into the room. She was carrying a small cardboard box.

A strange expression crossed Alejandrx's face; something like disappointment, and shx dropped Ben's hand quickly.

Reina came over to the table and set down the box. "I found them."

She removed a series of small black sacks, cinched shut so that they resembled a set of bean bags. She undid the tie on one and shook a strange tangle of metal and wires out onto the table. She handed it to Alejandrx, who unfurled a wired glove. Shx slipped it over hxr hand and held it up for Ben to see.

By then Reina had removed another from its sack. "This is for you. Let me help you."

Ben offered his hand. Reina carefully slipped the complex network of nodes and wires over his fingers, bringing the elastic cinch to his wrist. The glove was delicate, almost weightless. He ran his hand gingerly over the table, then through his beard. It was like a second skin.

"They're resilient," Reina said. She took one of the sacks, tossed it into the air and watched as it crashed the floor ten feet away. "Almost nothing you can't do with them, except...you know."

She grinned. It took Ben a moment to register her insinuation, and he was frankly shocked by the vulgarity.

Alejandrx tipped hxr head back and laughed at his expression. While shx pulled on another glove, Reina removed from the box a plastic case, which contained several pairs of translucent glasses on rubbery stems, each set a different color: blue, green, red, orange. She dispersed these, together with a second glove, and then pulled on her own set.

Ben slipped the glasses into place and managed to get his other glove on without embarrassing himself.

—Estás lista?

The words, a bright clear green, appeared before his eyes, as if hovering a foot or so before his gaze, then shrank and took up space in the upper left corner of his view. Instinctively, Ben turned his eyes to see the words, and they expanded once again into his line of sight. After a moment, they receded again into the corner.

"What does that mean?"

—It means, are you ready?

Again, the words appeared before his eyes, lingered for a moment, then receded.

Ben turned to Alejandrx, who raised hxr hand and quickly made a series of signs.

As shx did so, the letters shx had taught Ben appeared before his eyes in bright red: $HELLO$. In a split second, they merged and became a word: *Hello*. Then they too slipped away. When he followed them, the entire conversation slipped back into view. He found that by looking up or down, the lines of text would shift their prominence.

—Try to spell something. Anything.

Ben wracked his mind for the letters to hello. Fairly straightforward: HA ... no, $ELLO$.

The word, clear and blue, corrected to Hello and joined the conversation.

"It's really...extraordinary."

—Very useful.

Ben turned to Alejandrx.

"This is how you spoke. In the bug suit."

—Bug suit?

"When you came for me in Queensborough. There was a voice."

—Bug suit. I love it!

This was in green. Reina. Ben turned to her. She was grinning.

"How much sign do I need to learn?"

Reina shook her head, but her expression remained friendly. She signed as easily as Alejandrx.

—Honey, you're going to need to keep up.

ten

THE NOVELTY OF being able to see the language that emerged from the signs made the process less painful than it might otherwise have been. Despite himself, he was enjoying the training. Reina brought out an otherwise hidden silly side in Alejandrx, for there was no subject into which she could not sneak some vulgarity or insinuation. No matter how often it happened, Ben found himself discombobulated, which invariably caused Alejandrx to snort with laughter.

—Breakfast is ready.

These letters came through in a pale gold.

Ben did his best to spell out his question: —Who seid …said that?

—Kiral, downstairs, Alejandrx responded. —All of the glasses are on the wireless.

"You have wireless?"

—Not for you!

Reina laughed hard at this, and Alejandrx broke out in a grin.

—Let's remove our gloves. You don't want them to get sticky.

A moment passed.

—If you know what I mean.

Aloud, Ben said, "I really don't."

"Well," Reina peeled off her gloves, tossed them unceremoniously onto the table. "We can't all be so lucky."

KIRAL WAS NOT there when they descended. She had set up a folding table with an electric kettle, a stack of paper cups, tea bags, a sack of ground coffee and a French Press. She had arranged platters of fruit—apples, bananas, kiwis, cherries—and between them a plate stacked high with some kind of holed bun.

"What's this?" Ben asked, raising one of the strange buns to examine it better. It was coated in a sprinkling of salt, seeds and charred chunks of something fragrant. Garlic?

"A bagel."

"A bagel?"

Reina was staring at him.

"Are you kidding me?"

She turned to Alejandrx: "He really doesn't know his holes."

"I would never consume this many complex carbohydrates in a single meal."

Reina began to laugh again. "Honey, you really are deprived. I'mma fix you up."

She took the bagel from him, sliced it in half, and spread it generously with a thick white cream. She handed it back to him on a plate.

"There you go, bagel with schmear."

"Schmear?"

"A schmear of cream cheese. Just try it. You'll fucking love it."

Ben took a bite. It was delicious, utterly unlike his usual breakfasts of protein blends and egg whites.

"It's quite good."

Alejandrx signed something that he did not catch. No, he remembered part of it.

—You have…

Shx reached over and wiped from his mustache a spot of the cream cheese.

"Not as effective as just licking it off," Reina said, sending herself into hysterics.

"Mr. Nakamura."

Kiral was standing at the top of the staircase by the conference room. He had not seen her ascend.

"Get something to drink, then join me here."

Ben used the lav, made himself a cup of jasmine green tea and went upstairs. Kiral had wiped down the board so that all signs of their morning were gone, as was the box that had contained the glasses and gloves. In its place was a laptop connected to an external hard drive.

"Take a seat." She had taken Alejandrx' place at the whiteboard. She, too, had a cup of tea, which she kept in her hands for warmth. The room was cold.

Ben sat gingerly. His fingers ached to pry open the laptop. He waited for the catch.

"The computer is not connected to the internet." There it was. "It has substantially lower computing power than its size would suggest. The hard drive is encrypted by an early version of the code Villaseñor is likely to be running."

"Gordian.knot."

Kiral nodded. Ben gnawed a little as his lower lip. Gordian.knot was ancient—by internet standards, anyway. Villaseñor had developed it as a teenager, when Ben was still in primary school. It was the work that had put him on the map, a flex to show that he was more than just hereditary scion, more, even, than a well-taught, intelligent hacker, another in a long line of Villaseñors. He, like the founder of his clan, was a genius.

Even Ben had to admit it.

The encryption took its name from the infamous knot of Gordium. Perched in an ox cart and consisting of many knots tied together so tightly that their parts had become indistinguishable, the Gordian Knot awaited the one who could undo it, and thus conquer all Asia.

The innovation of the Gordian.knot code was that it was laid out apparently plain as day to be decrypted, except that the lines of code had been sliced up and rearranged so completely that nobody had been able to write a script that could "untangle" it.

A line might run for one or two or three thousand characters, then meet with an abrupt syntax change that denoted another logical operation elsewhere in the code. A scan of the remaining code might reveal a plausible continuation, except that even as the script "patched" the two lines together, the rest of the code would rearrange itself, like so much of its namesake's rope.

Many people had tried to untangle the Gordian Knot, and all had failed.

So too with what was known among the hacker class now only as "dot knot."

Ben himself had spent hours tinkering with the various iterations Villaseñor had released over the years. As if the beta were not robust enough. Ben was unaware of any successful function to handle a dot knot decryption.

That didn't mean one didn't exist. Ernő Rubik himself had despaired of solving the puzzle that bore his name.

"Can I conduct research?"

"I presume you mean online? No. It is too risky."

"Risky? To browse the web?"

Kiral thought for a moment. "Imagine you find something online, something resembling a solution. Do you think Villaseñor has failed to set up AI's to report back to him on traffic around the messageboards? Imagine he has. There is a sudden burst of activity around solving the Gordian.knot problem. What is the first thing he is likely to assume?"

Ben sat for a long time thinking. Kiral said nothing.

"This is an early version?"

"The first."

"It's likely to be very different now. Villaseñor has never stopped tinkering."

"Amina is trying to get you a version of the live code."

Ben laughed. Except Kiral wasn't joking.

"There is another limitation."

"What now?"

"We travel light, Mr. Nakamura. Your solution will need to fit on this."

She set another drive on the desk beside him. He picked it up. It was ostentatiously old-school. No touch screen. Retractable port wiring. It had a single-button interface. The idea was simple—you connected, hit the button, and let the program work its magic.

"How big?"

She told him.

He leaned back in his chair. "You want me to break the world's most intractable code using an algorithm with the computing power of a twenty-first century cellphone?"

"Do you think you can travel with a quantum computer on your back?" Kiral cocked her head. "We know what works, Mr. Nakamura. You're the one who insisted on going along."

ELEVEN

B EN HAD TINKERED with dot knot before, but never on such a paltry machine. It was a kind of mortification, a reminder of his limitations as a hacker. He made no progress and quickly grew sullen.

At one point that day, Kiral returned to invite him to lunch. He had snapped at her, and she had left without another word.

Hours later, he noticed that someone had placed a plate of food, a fresh cup of tea, on the table. He had been too engrossed in the work to see who.

He ate ravenously, and swallowed the tea, now cold, in a few greedy gulps.

It was not his fault he had snapped. What were they expecting, asking him to work under these conditions? He should at least be able to play around with a solution on a stronger machine…it bothered him that he knew she was right about the risks of research online.

He knew it was the convocation of the clans that weighed on him. Every moment that passed ticked off another second on the doomsday clock that counted down the hours 'til his humiliation. That his day had passed quickly for all of its fruitlessness, was a bitter harbinger of the days to come.

He closed the laptop roughly and descended to the warehouse.

Hong and Reina were in the middle of the warehouse, bickering with one another over something he couldn't follow.

Ben went in search of food, saw Alejandrx out of the corner of his eye, but shx was busy with something, and he didn't interrupt.

Amina appeared from the downstairs room, dressed in skintight black from head to toe. She acknowledged him with a nod, then went to where Reina and Hong had disappeared behind the Descartes Room.

They had affixed a length of chain link fence along one side of the platform. The air began to thrum and the base of the Descartes platform began to rise up on its posts, so that they rested underneath it like legs. The fence rose too. Ben walked over to where they were still bickering.

"Did you connect the hydraulic valve?"

"Of course!"

"Then you explain why it isn't working."

Hong gave a huff and knelt beside a long narrow platform that rested on a row of thick black rubber balloons along the fenced side of the Descartes Room.

"So now you believe me?" Reina said.

"No, I'm proving my point." He reached under the platform and gave a few strenuous jerks. "There."

He rose, wiped his hands on his suit pants, leaving a grease stain.

"So I was right!"

"No. The hydraulic valve was coupled. The cable was jammed under the brace."

Reina rolled her eyes.

"Que Dios me dé serenidad," she muttered.

Hong pointedly ignored her and climbed onto the platform. He pressed a pedal at his feet. There was a hissing sound, and the platform gave a tremble.

When he saw Ben, he waved him over.

"Be my guinea pig. Come, get on the boat."

"Boat?"

"The—the platform. Imagine it's a boat."

Ben cracked his neck and stepped gingerly onto the platform. It sank under his weight, and he nearly lost his balance. It was easier to stand with both feet on board.

"Okay."

"Now wait a moment, while I input a wave function."

Hong pressed the pedal a few more times.

The platform began to bob and sway on the synthetic tide of the rubber balloons. Ben's knee gave way, but he caught himself, and in a moment had his sea legs. He had spent considerable time sailing in his youth.

Alejandrx reappeared now. Like Amina, shx was clad in skintight black.

Ben began to descend from the platform.

"Where do you think you're going?" Reina chided him.

"Are we not finished? This isn't for tomorrow?"

"Are you tired, Mr. Nakamura?" Amina.

"Yes. Quite. Radical honesty and all that."

He was jittery tired, lines of code dancing before his eye one moment, thoughts of home the next. His neck hurt, his back hurt, his eyes throbbed. He was discouraged by the day's utter lack of progress with dot knot. He wanted a hot shower. He couldn't believe he was functioning on four and a half hours of sleep.

And yet, he could not wait to tackle the cipher again tomorrow.

"I'm afraid our timetable demands long days. Have you worked out what we are doing?"

"Why don't you tell me?" His tone was sharper than

he'd intended. He was tired of the elliptical answers.

Amina made a sour expression. "I will. As you know, the consulates are surrounded on three sides by security walls. Insurmountable. To approach from the sky is inadvisable, for obvious reasons. That leaves the river."

Of course. The riverside was less fortified, partly because river travel was so dangerous, but also because consulate staff used the stretch of greenway that ran the length of Old Yorktown to lunch, and they enjoyed the view.

"That's quite a jump." Ben reached for the bottom edge of the platform. He was easily a foot short on tiptoes.

"I'm still trying to figure out the tides," Reina interjected. "Hong, the archivist, thinks you'll be closer. I, the career operations analyst, think farther. But here's the deal: you'll come down the river. You're going to catch yourselves on one of the barge moorings and hold tight while Mobo works his magic. Then, one by one, you're going to get from the boat to the ledge, and then you'll have eight seconds to scale the fence before the electricity comes back on."

"The fence is electric?"

Reina raised her eyebrow. "It's not cotton candy."

Ben sighed.

"What happens if it doesn't work?"

"What?"

"You said if Mobo's magic works. What happens if it doesn't?"

"You go on to resolve Pascal's wager."

Reina pulled a stopwatch from her pocket. "Eight seconds. Who's first?"

Amina and Alejandrx turned to Ben. "Will you need some assistance?"

Ben scowled. "I should think not."

Amina's eyebrow began to rise, but she suppressed it. "Then it will be me."

She and Alejandrx ascended the "boat," kneeling down at either end. Ben knelt too. His calves ached from sitting all day. He was never this inert in Manahatta.

"I'll give you the signal, hit the timer. Eight seconds later, you need to be on the other side of the fence."

"Can you give us a count?"

"Yes. On three. One. Two. Three." Reina clicked the stopwatch. It was a strangely long time. When the eight seconds had elapsed, Reina clicked the stopwatch. "That's it. Up, down. Done. Ready?"

"Wait. Will each of us have eight seconds?"

"Good question. Mobo is going to rig it so that the system fails six times at staggered intervals."

"And how will we know it's failing?"

"We'll be wired the whole time. One of us will walk you through it."

"No, I mean how will we know you're correct?"

"You're just going to have to trust Mobo."

"Are we quite finished? I am shortest, so I will need a hand." Amina moved to the center of the boat and rose to a squat. Alejandrx came up alongside her.

"Go!" Reina yelled.

Immediately, Alejandrx bent hxr arms to create a platform for Amina's foot. Amina rose from her crouch, planted a foot firmly in Alejandrx's arms, and with a boost from Alejandrx, leapt the distance to the rim of the platform. She lost her balance for a moment but stabilized herself by planting her feet against the "wall" of the platform. With a grunt, she managed to pull herself up so that she was standing alongside the fence. She grabbed it, and raised a foot, but Reina yelled, "Two…one."

Amina let go of the fence, and stood, arms outstretched, waiting for Reina to give her the signal that it was safe to climb. After a moment, however, she lost her balance, and fell backwards. Alejandrx moved like lightning to cushion her fall, and Amina managed to land without breaking anything. She shook her head at the failed attempt, but she was smiling.

"Soaking wet," Reina shouted. "Back of the line."

Alejandrx knelt and again made a cradle of hxr arms. Shx indicated that Ben should use hxr for a boost.

He shook his head and indicated that shx should go first. Alejandrx pursed hxr lips momentarily, then rose to a squat. Shx turned to Reina for the signal. When it came, shx leapt straight up, gripping the lip of the platform with the tips of hxr fingers. In a single motion, shx pulled hxrself to the platform, and then instantly leapt half the height of the fence. Shx scrambled it like a squirrel, and at the top, shx propelled hxrself over feet first. Shx dropped then as if suspended by a rope, first halfway down the fence, then to the inner platform, landing without a sound. Shx rose to hxr full height and jerked hxr head to Reina.

"Six seconds."

Alejandrx grinned and shook out hxr shoulders and knees.

"Mr. Nakamura, you're up."

Impressive as Alejandrx had appeared, Ben was sure he could match hxr. Like many of his peers, good breeding and long hours of training had turned him into an elite athlete, a Kendo champion, with national titles and a bronze medal at the Olympics, taken on the second of his three journeys to the Games. Though he had retired from the competitive circuit in anticipation of his ascension, he had maintained his training regimen. That morning was the first time in more than a decade that he had not begun the day in the gymnasium.

He bent his knees, tried to gauge the force he'd need to get to the platform. Would he try to take the same path that Alejandrx—

"Go!"

It caught him off guard. A momentary setback. Ben fired his legs, shot up towards the platform. He managed to grab the edge, but he had not anticipated the texture—already in his mind, he had turned the thing into rough concrete.

What his fingers met was the strange smooth material of the Descartes Room floor. He lost his grip and landed hard on flat feet.

"Fuck." His ankle hurt. He turned gingerly, hoping it was just the shock of the fall and not something more serious.

Amina was already back on the platform. Alejandrx had swung back down, to take hxr place beside Amina.

"Nakamura! What the hell are you waiting for? Back of the line."

TWELVE

BEN HAD NO idea what time they had returned to the apartment—Amina had flown back with him in a VTOL. She had gone right to bed, but Ben had stood over the table stuffing a plate of cold food into his mouth. Beyond that, he remembered almost nothing.

They had drilled for God knows how long. He could feel the lingering smart of his ankle. Of the three, Ben was the only one who hadn't made the climb in under eight seconds.

Ben changed and went out to the kitchen. Amina and Kiral were already there, eating toast and tea. Amina indicated that he should help himself.

"We will travel together this morning." It was Amina who spoke.

Kiral avoided his gaze.

After breakfast, Kiral tidied. Then they headed to the roof. In half a minute a cab descended out of the fog.

"I've forgotten something," Amina said.

"We can wait," Kiral said.

Ben blushed with shame for his behavior yesterday. He didn't think he could bear to be alone with her.

Amina waved them into the cab. "I will catch you up. Go, get started."

So they rode together, Kiral seated across from him, her gaze locked on the view through the window.

He knew that she was hurt. It was a strange feeling to see it in another person, worse to know that it was his doing. What he could not imagine was how to make it right. He was not one to apologize. His world bent around him.

Yet he could not ignore her pain.

"I—"

Kiral kept her head bent away from him.

"I regret that I was rude. Yesterday."

A strange expression passed over her, an interior wind. She turned to meet his gaze.

"Thank you."

She turned her eyes back to the window.

"I have always hated to fly. That is why I watch. I have to assure myself that we are still airborne."

"And are we?"

"For now."

ALEJANDRX RAISED AN eyebrow when shx saw that it was just the two of them.

"Amina is on her way," Kiral said, signing as she spoke. "I'm going to go inside."

Alejandrx nodded. Ben started after Kiral, but Alejandrx indicated with a quick waggle of her finger that he should pause. Shx too started to sign.

It took Ben a moment to catch up with her. Shx was signing…the alphabet! He nodded and raised his own hand. He began with an S, but corrected himself quickly. *A B C D*…he was mostly there. When he botched the thumb position for M, shx took his hand in hxrs, showed him to start from the pinky, and proceed inwards to the index finger. *M… N…* and *T*.

He had just finished the alphabet, when Alejandrx quickly signed: *L O O K U P*.

A second VTOL was descending through the rose of early morning. Amina greeted them a moment later, pecking Alejandrx on both cheeks. "Shall we?"

She started off at a jog. Alejandrx indicated that Ben should follow. He started after Amina, relieved, allowing himself to ease into the run. The stiffness of his muscles' resistance quickly wore away, and he entered the delicious stage of the run where his body's thirst for exercise was sated.

He thought at first that it was just him and Amina running, for he heard no sound of Alejandrx. Yet when he turned his head to cast a quick glance over his shoulder, there shx was, paced about as far behind him as he was to Amina.

He thought he might do a little showing off—after all, what had he trained for all those decades if not for physical glory? He picked up his pace, hoping to overtake Amina in a minute or two.

Yet the distance between them remained constant. Ben increased his pace again, his stride slightly longer. Still Amina maintained her distance. A glance over the shoulder confirmed that Alejandrx too had come up to match his speed.

Once more he accelerated, and for the third time he found his position between them unchanged. He decided now that he would, if nothing else, grind them down through sheer stamina. They were running quickly now. He knew he could maintain the pace for an hour.

They were running through an industrial neighborhood, long avenues running between warehouses, some so old as to be brick. There was the smell of brackish water, sharp and salty, and in places, the water had come up to run in little creeks through the cracked and uneven concrete.

They turned a corner, following now the long winding curve of Old Breuckelen's seaside border. The water shone grey and white in the morning light, and out to sea he could make out the faint ochre floodlights of cargo ships anchored in the outer harbor.

They had been running for half an hour, and the sun was up. It was warm now, and Ben had begun to sweat. The sweetness of the run had peaked and he was now caught up in the anxieties that crowded in despite his best efforts to keep his focus on the run.

To clear his head, he decided on a whim to go off trail. They were running past a copse of residential towers, arranged in a rough semicircle around a tidy green-space, a playground and a dog run. Ben broke across the green, leaping a low fence and aiming for the lane between the buildings.

It was easier to run across the grass and he picked up his pace. Curious, he cast another look behind him.

Alejandrx was cutting the hypotenuse to the lane so quickly he had little doubt shx would beat him there. More incredible, when shx saw that he had spotted hxr, shx winked at him, and when shx came upon the swing set, rather than pass between the swings, shx jumped two-footed over the seat, between the chains, and landed in stride.

Ben lost pleasure at his transgression and slowed his pace. Alejandrx came up beside him, and like a sheepdog, set a course at his elbow that brought him back into line behind Amina, who had paused ahead to watch. They caught up with her and paused. Amina was breathing heavily.

"I wasn't really going to run."

"I didn't think you were," Amina replied.

Ben took a deep breath, allowed the lactic acid to wash from his system.

Alejandrx was not even out of breath.

thirteen

THE DAYS DEVELOPED a rhythm. Runs long enough to wear him out. Five minutes for a lukewarm shower in the warehouse lav. Sign language drills, lunch, taken together, Ben too exhausted to join in the others' laughter. He grinded it all out because in the afternoons, they left him alone with dot knot.

He had made no progress. None. Every single tack he took met with the absolute impenetrability of the code. He would find something for his digital fingertips to hold on to, and he could follow it, sometimes for hours, only to find that he had doubled back on a double back, and was now ensnared in a random tangle of logic streams, neither closer nor farther from his starting point. Because what was a starting point in that warped tangled mess?

He might have been angry. Furious, even. The convocation of the clans loomed, Damoclean. He was ensnared in his rival's greatest accomplishment—the same rival who would be giddiest to supersede him among the peers.

Yet there was clarity in his purpose. When he was mired in the code, all other considerations fell away. There was no thought of the convocation—no thought of Amina and her crew, the madness of their mission to retrieve Matsukata's blade. He was a world class Kendo master. Yet even at the height of his prowess, he had never achieved the clarity in Kendo that he found in the labyrinth of the knot.

Yet when, at the end of every day, he heard footsteps ascending the staircase, he could only close his eyes and make peace at the humiliation of failure.

Failures.

He was still the only one of the three who had not ascended the fence in time. Most of the time, he could get a rhythm going as he ascended. But every time he thought he had it beat, he was yanked from his reverie by Reina's reverberating cry: "Dead!"

"Dead! Dead! Dead!"

He had made the mistake of complaining—once.

"This is absurd. I've been awake how long. Sixteen hours? Eighteen? And I'm supposed to do this?"

Reina gave a barking laugh. "You think you're going to do this on a good night's sleep and a full stomach? Use your goddam brain, Nakamura. You're going to need to do this off a real boat with your fingertips flop-sweating with adrenaline. We aren't doing this to make you feel stupid. We're making sure you can do it when the pressure's on and there's no room for fucking up."

Ben had lowered his eyes, but he raised them to glance at Alejandrx. Shx was signing something to Hong, who nodded and gave a low snort of laughter. It took a moment before Ben realized that he had understood. Shx had said, "It doesn't hurt."

He flushed with anger and shame. He was unused to being outmatched.

From Villaseñor he could handle it. Villaseñor was a peer.

Alejandrx was…what?

Shx was gifted. He could not deny it. What shx did came more easily to hxr than anything had ever come to him. He could recognize hxr genius.

He had worked like a dog for his successes. It was the price paid for his station. He was proud that his work had paid off, proud that it was work that had earned his successes, in school, Kendo, his coding.

After all, a dynastic clan could not rely on accidents of history.

He resolved, in a moment of bile, to find hxr weakness. Show Alejandrx that shx laughed at him at hxr peril.

Ben's mind was unquiet, a tangle of frustrations.

He squatted on aching thighs before the bookshelf in his room. He could read; that would distract him, he hoped. Settle his mind for sleep.

He scanned the shelf. He was uninterested in the economic theory, too tired for political philosophy. There was no fiction, but there was history—Herodotus and Thucydides, and, there on the far side, his old friend, Plutarch. He drew it from the shelf and flipped to the tables of contents.

It had to be a coincidence—but there it was, in the seventh volume of the *Lives*, the *Life of Alexander*.

The Gordian Knot was a cultural cliché—everyone knew the story of how Alexander, destined to conquer Asia, used his sword to cut open the knot. Yet Villaseñor was a classicist. There were any number of intractable puzzles or mathematical formulations he might have used for his code's namesake. He had chosen this one.

Ben lay back on the bed, the slim green book in his hand. He stretched his calves and began to read.

It was there in the early pages of the text:

> ... and after he had taken the city of
> Gordium, reputed to have been the home of
> the ancient Midas, he saw the much-talked-
> of waggon bound fast to its yoke with the bark
> of the cornel-tree, and heard a story confidently
> told about it by the Barbarians, to the effect that
> whosoever loosed the fastening was destined
> to become king of the whole world. Well, then,
> most writers say that since the fastenings had
> their ends concealed, and were intertwined many
> times in crooked coils, Alexander was at a loss
> how to proceed, and finally loosened the knot by
> cutting it through with his sword, and that when
> it was thus smitten many ends were to be seen.

Ben chuckled. If only it were so easy. He had never thought about what the knot was for—to keep an old wagon tied up. He had always imagined the knot as a carnival exhibition: a massive freestanding knot on a stage, open to anyone of ambition to test his destiny.

He was surprised by the next line:

> But Aristobulus says that he undid it very easily,
> by simply taking out the so-called "hestor,"
> *or pin*, of the waggon-pole, by which the yoke-
> fastening was held together, and then drawing
> away the yoke.

Ben lay still for a long time.

fourteen

BEN BOOTED UP the laptop with a racing heart. If a single line reference to Aristobulus proffered a metaphorical skeleton key—and he doubted less and less—then he needn't untangle the code. That was a fool's errand, every tug a tightening of another loop. Nor should he seek for some kind of sword—any "cut" to the code would cause the lines to rupture, perhaps even irrecoverably, and in that was a kind of fail safe.

No. There must be a lynchpin. His task now was to find it.

He had spoken not a word that morning over breakfast with Mobo and Kiral, the VTOL ride, the run through Sunset Park, apace with the women who flanked him.

"You are contemplative this morning, Mr. Nakamura," Amina said when they arrived back at the warehouse. She mopped the sweat from her forehead with a towel and handed around a bottle of water. Alejandrx drank deep, handed off to Ben.

"I hardly slept."

"I know the feeling well. We are close. How are you feeling?"

She wasn't usually this chatty. Was she building to something? Softening him up? Perceptive enough to sense that he may just have figured it out? He doubted he was the only one with secrets.

He could not tell whether Alejandrx was paying them any attention.

Ben was excited to shower and change, but to his surprise, they found Hong and Reina in the center of the warehouse setting up the Descartes Room and arguing over where to lay the mess of cables. Hong looked up at the sound of them.

"I—er—have good news and bad."

Ben glanced at Amina, who had stepped aside to confer with Reina.

"The good news is, Villaseñor has constructed an illegal atrium on the river side of the consulate. The bad news, that means, well obviously, it has—the fact is we aren't sure yet of the implications on security."

"I don't follow," Ben said.

Hong took a deep breath, as if winding up for a lecture.

"We've been drilling for a top entry. We know there's a rooftop interface for you to—well, you know. We don't know whether there is one through the atrium. If there isn't, well, then that's just handy spandy, Jacky Dandy, but if there's an alternative security apparatus, all your work is for naught."

"Why not just stick to the original plan? Do the roof descent?"

Alejandrx cleared hxr throat. Shx signed, and to his delight, Ben found that he could piece together much of what shx said. "How high is the atrium?"

"One point five stories."

Alejandrx shrugged. —That's easier.

"If the security system is the same."

—It's the same to me.

Amina came over now and put a hand on Hong's shoulder.

"You're over-worrying. I will see what they have."

"How?" This was the part Ben understood least of all.

"It's not something you need to worry about. But it means I will need to be gone this afternoon. Let's run the drills now, instead."

Ben stifled the urge to resist. Dot knot could wait.

He and Alejandrx got the "boat" into place while Hong and Reina rigged up the fence. They were about to begin when Kiral came in with a rolling metal suitcase.

"I hope I'm not interrupting."

To Ben's surprise, she rose to her tiptoes and met Amina's lips in a quick kiss. Ah, he thought. Of course.

"Is it ready?"

Kiral nodded.

Amina clapped her hands with pleasure. "Wonderful. Let's show Mr. Nakamura."

Ben stepped down from the boat. The change in routine had him skittish, and he had the sense that everything going on was an elaborate performance.

He shook off the thought. Unless they could read minds, there was no way they could know that he suspected he could beat the dot knot. Amina had said it: they were simply getting close. The stakes were high for all of them.

Kiral set the suitcase on its side and undid the clasps. Inside was a neatly folded set of black clothes. She handed them to Ben, then took out a second, smaller case and a lightweight black armored vest.

"Why don't you dress?"

"What's in the little case?"

"Dress first."

THE SUIT FIT perfectly. It was unlike anything Ben had ever felt, lightweight and pliant, sturdy and supportive. He rolled his shoulders, bent at the waist. The fabric moved with him, as if it were intuitive. The armored vest was the same, slightly awkward to buckle without help, but once in place, immediately forgotten.

He returned to the warehouse floor to find that Amina and Alejandrx too had dressed in the armored suits.

"You've seen these before," Kiral said. She had sprung the latch on the smaller case and was handing around the pairs of gloves. "The wiring has been stitched into the fabric, but the mechanism is the same. These are yours."

Ben took the pair of black gloves and slipped them over his hands. Unlike the pair they had demonstrated for him on the first day at the warehouse, there was no sense of the underlying technology. He flexed and extended his fingers several times.

"These will work the same way?"

Kiral nodded. "The glasses have been integrated into your suit, too."

"The glasses?"

Alejandrx came up behind him. For a moment he felt hxr fingers at the back of his neck. He reached back instinctively, and shx placed a thin fold of fabric into his fingers. He turned to see hxr pull a snug black hood over hxr head. Hxr eyes were now covered by the shiny red goggles, and there was a tidy hole over hxr mouth.

Ben pulled his own mask on. The world was ever so slightly tinged in blue.

—Looking good.

The words appeared in red before his eyes, then swooped neatly into the upper left corner of his view.

"There's just one more piece." Kiral opened a final box to reveal a bed of charcoal foam, in which were set six circular pieces of metal. Kiral handed them out.

Alejandrx and Amina set the apparatus into their mouths. Ben imitated them. The interior rim was lined with a strip of soft silicone that adjusted imperceptibly to the bite of his teeth.

"There is one wire to connect," Kiral said. She adjusted something on Ben's mouthpiece. "The suit is run through with microtubing filled with an ultracool compound. It will regulate the temperature in the suit, so that you don't cook. How do you feel?"

Ben started to remove the apparatus from his mouth, thought better of it, and signed, —It is good. Feels good.

His words appeared in blue, then settled into the chat stream below Alejandrx's.

He turned to hxr. It was the first time since his arrival that he had seen Alejandrx in the bug suit. Shx and Amina stood side-by-side, and in the black suits, they were variations on a mutant arthropod drone. The only distinguishing feature now was the color of their eyes, red and green.

"Now that you're, ah, ready, I'm going to load the atrium sub-parcel." Hong punched something into the control panel, and the Descartes Room began to shift and adjust. "We're working backwards now, so we're going to rebuild your muscle memory."

Ben no longer needed to be facing Amina to see her words.

—Let's get on the boat.

He was alone in the office, laptop open, dot knot one-point-oh running through the drive.

Ben leaned back, sipped his jasmine green tea, contemplated the jet-black interface with its flickering emerald cursor.

He needed to unlearn everything about the dot knot architecture. Heart pounding, he cleared the memory, tossing every line of script, all the arcane logic that had enabled him to pry at the tangle of code that stood between him and Matsukata's blade.

His job was not to untangle the knot. He needed to find the lynchpin.

The lynchpin was a metaphor, of course. But what in the name of the dog did it mean?

Dot knot was an illusion, like one of the heirloom puzzle boxes his Syrian grandmother had given him and his sisters as children, perfect in their self-containment. And yet there was always a trick that would unlock the box, a simple movement, and the solution would be, in retrospect, perfectly obvious.

The impossible complexity of dot knot was a sleight of hand to distract from the solution, and it was as much a psychological game as anything else. Villaseñor would know that any hacker worthy of the code would pride himself on his ability to unwind it, and their hubris was the surest way to entrust to the perfection of its secret.

Ben leaned forward. He would run a scout program, probe the contours, only this time, he would try to look not at but *through* the picture that emerged.

He breathed deep.

FIFTEEN

THE WAREHOUSE WAS empty, the lights low. Ben had a vague memory of being interrupted at one point, a stronger sense that whoever it had been had understood that he was not to be disturbed.

He wondered for a moment whether he was alone, but there was a sound from the office below. He descended the stairs and called hello, but there was no response.

If it were Alejandrx, it would be fruitless to call out. He hoped it was shx.

He decided to try the downstairs door. He was about to knock when there was a loud clap behind him. He spun on his heels.

—What are you doing?
—I'm done. I thought I heard someone.
—You can't go in there.
—I was looking for you.
Alejandrx smiled.
—I'm teasing you. Amina would keep no secret here.
Ben was not sure how to respond.

—Come on, I'm tired. You are keeping me up too late.

They locked up and went outside. It was the darkest Ben had ever seen the place, the totemic streetlights arching high overhead casting only sickly light.

There was a whirr of air and a squall of dust and paper. A VTOL came sinking deftly through the sour darkness. Alejandrx climbed up first, offered Ben hxr hand.

The doors slid closed, and the cab ascended. Alejandrx, across from him, leaned back in hxr seat and closed hxr eyes. Ben too began to drift. When he woke from the lurch of his stomach at their descent, he found that their legs were entwined. Alejandrx was watching him, and when shx saw that he too was awake, shx did not move.

He had assumed that shx would escort him back and then flutter moth-like into the night.

Instead, while he stood at the kitchen sink drinking a glass of water, shx went to the linen closet for bedding and a pillow. Shx returned to the living room and began to fix up the low green couch.

When shx glanced his way, he asked her, "You don't intend to sleep on the couch?"

—Where else should I sleep?

—I have a bed.

—Large enough for two?

Ben was tired. The implication came to him only after a moment. He blushed. It had not occurred to him, and he protested.

—I meant that you should have it.

A soft, sad smile crossed hxr face, and shx turned back to the couch, tucking the sheet into the cushions. Ben regretted his rashness, but hxr response had confused him. Was shx truly insinuating that they should sleep together?

He felt a strange tightening in his belly at the thought, a want he had not had the temerity yet to acknowledge.

Having acknowledged it to himself, he did not know whether he could recover the possibility.

He went to the couch, began to help. Alejandrx stood back and watched his ineffectual attempts to spread the cover smooth.

After a moment, Ben too stopped.

—Please take the bed, he spelled laboriously.

—I don't want your chivalry. It's…

Shx signed a word he did not know, so shx spelled it. *Patronizing.*

—Not that. Courtesy. For another week, this is my home. You're my guest. Take the bed.

Shx mulled his response.

—Show me the way.

As if she did not know. Ben's spirits rose. Shx was asking him to come with hxr! He started for the bedroom, then thought better of it and snagged the pillow from the couch.

Alejandrx went into the bedroom, and to Ben's surprise turned and began to close the door. When shx saw that he was carrying the pillow, shx wrinkled hxr brow and looked him over.

Ben blushed again.

—The other pillow, it's…not as nice as this.

There, again, the cryptic smile. Shx went to the bed, removed the pillow, and swapped with Ben in the doorway, the pillows alone crossing the threshold.

—Good night, shx signed, and again began to close the door.

Ben felt the possibility of night foreclosing upon him, and on an impulse reached out a hand to stay the door.

"One more thing," he said aloud, watching hxr eyes as shx read his lips.

Shx waited expectantly for him to finish.

Could he ask hxr for what he wanted? What he had been sure shx wanted too?

No. He would be mortified by the faux pas, and besides that, it was impossible to imagine the mission after such a breach. He felt every inch a fool.

Except for one thing, the secret he had held close until now.

"I broke the code."

Sixteen

There had been a lynchpin.

The encryption algorithm was a tangle, but he had realized as he conducted scan after scan after scan that it was not unevenly messy. There were consistent sets of interpretable string, some longer, others shorter, but these lengths tended to repeat periodically. Having seen this aspect of the code, he could not unsee it. The periodicity must point to some meta context—the lynchpin—but because the code reconstituted itself at each shift in the interpretability, he was left without any sense of what it meant.

He was eight hours into the afternoon's work, and that on top of the morning's training in the big suit. His eyes were watery, his tongue dry.

He reached for his tea—empty. The tea bag, long since drained of flavor, sat in a dish beside his cup. The tag had come loose: *Jasmine Green Tea—Product of Zhao Sinecure*. Ben picked it up absentmindedly to fidget with while he worked, folding it first along the center, then down from each corner so that their tips met in the center.

Bored and frustrated, he tossed it aside. It landed flat, one of the corners up at a perpendicular angle.

Ben stared at it for a long time.

And then he saw it. With trembling fingers, he reached for the tag. The brew instructions on the back were visible in displaced quarters. Ben turned the tag over and over, his mind whirring.

Could it be? It was a mathematical contrivance of the highest order, simple—but brilliant in its simplicity.

What if the code had been laid out two-dimensionally, and then "folded" into the shape it now took? The breaks in the syntax, then, were places that the code had been folded. And the folding was intricate, so that guessing wrong meant further folding…

It was a contrivance of course—the code was no more two dimensional than it was one—but Ben understood that if he was right, dot knot could be disentangled by code that could instruct it on how to unfold.

This was an entirely new puzzle, far outside Ben's ken. He was no mathematician.

He decided to begin by cataloguing the nodes where the code "bent." That would give him a sense of how to write the parameters for where a decrypt algorithm should "unfold."

He wrote a script to scan for nodes and feed the results into the outline of an algorithm. Start here, then go here, then here…

But what to do at each *here*?

Since he had no intuition into the shape of the folds, he decided to tell the program to try a series of unfoldings, a statistical distribution of options he could append to a series of nested Bayesian instructions so that the program would learn what had worked and then begin that set of unfoldings at the next node.

It would take a long time to run because of the low computer power, but it would work. And if it didn't, the error reports would give him a foothold for the next program.

He wrote for an hour, then ran the code. The first time it hit a node, it kicked back errors, and he nearly cried, but he saw that it was a syntax error he'd overlooked in his exhaustion, and quickly fixed it.

Then he ran it again.

"And it worked?"

"It worked."

Amina and Kiral exchanged an impenetrable glance. Ben was standing before the laptop.

"If you look here," he pointed to the screen, "you can see that the full script executed, which means that it hit no snags. It read the whole program. It can read dot knot."

"I am impressed, Mr. Nakamura," Kiral said. "We placed a great deal of hope in you. I'm glad to see we were right."

"How long does it take?" Amina.

"To run the decrypt?"

She nodded.

"This is not a decrypt, it's a read code. The decrypt will be taught from the results of the read. But, to answer your question, right now, the current iteration of the read takes two hours."

"We won't have—"

"I know," he interrupted. "But it's a learning algorithm. The more I train it, the faster it will get. And I'm not worried about the decrypt. This is the hard part."

"And how will you train it?"

"There are dozens of iterations online. Villaseñor has been releasing updates for years."

"What do you need from me?"

Ben tapped the hard drive with the original code. "Whoever gave you this—ask for more."

AMINA DID, RETURNING with a dozen more dot knots. Ben spent hours running his read code, sketching the outline of the decrypt on the whiteboard, swearing at errors, refining the code, untangling his own jangled logic. It took nine of the dozen to do it, but he managed to pare down the read time to under two minutes.

He could not help but wish to show off. He called everyone upstairs to huddle around his laptop. Only Amina could not be found.

Ben had two stacks of drives on the table beside the laptop. To the right, the dot knots he had untangled. To the left, the remaining three.

"I want to set the stage," he said. "The code that Villaseñor wrote has been floating around since its creation, free to access, a challenge to the world: has he created unbreakable encryption technology? He was flaunting it. I mean, Villaseñor uses this code to protect his own sinecure."

The others waited appreciatively.

"Mathematicians and computer scientists have tried for years, but so far every attempt to break it has failed." Ben grinned. "Until now."

Hong and Reina exchanged a glance which Ben ignored. Alejandrx's expression was a mask of curious bemusement. He decided to shut up and get on with it.

"I've written an algorithm capable of performing the decryption in minutes. I have never tested it on these drives. I'm going to do them now."

There was a moment of awkward silence.

"How will we know? That it's worked?"

"The algorithm won't return any errors."

"And that's enough to unlock it?"

"Good question. No, I still need to write the code to overwrite the security but that's—I wasn't going to get anywhere until—"

They had no idea what he had accomplished. He could go down in history alongside Turing and Rejewski, and here he was having to explain why he wasn't absolutely finished…

Embarrassed by his own enthusiasm, he plugged in the first of the three hard drives. Then he ran his script.

The first drive took six minutes, the second three.

The last he broke in thirty-seven seconds.

HONG AND REINA congratulated him and made their way downstairs.

Alejandrx squeezed Ben's shoulder.

—It's a very good job. I wish I could understand it better.

"Thank you."

Kiral remained to talk logistics.

"What's left to finalize it?"

"I need to know what the interface is, and I need a day to write the unlock code out of the lynchpin pull."

"Lynchpin pull?"

"Don't worry about it. There's three codes. One to read, one to decrypt, and one to use the results to disable the security."

Kiral nodded but her mind was elsewhere. She was absently chewing at the inside of her lower lip.

"You're sure the code will work?"

"Why?"

"Because there isn't really another option. There's no other way to breach the consulate."

"How recent are the dot knots?"

"Some of them are quite old."

Ben's high was quickly spoiling.

"It would really be best to have a newer version. As new as possible."

"What about the current version?"

Ben had not heard Amina on the stairs. She stood leaning against the door jamb.

"Do you really have it?"

Amina nodded. She looked tired. Tired and serious. His pleasure at breaking the code was now utterly usurped by anxiety.

"I feel like there's something you're not telling me."

"No, nothing. It is too late for secrets."

She came to hand over another drive. Ben booted up the interface. With trembling fingers he executed the decrypt script.

His heart crashed.

SEVENTEEN

REINA AND HONG, seated across from him in the VTOL, chatted about the difficulty Hong had procuring a certain glue for restoring the bindings of old books, the sailboat Reina's grandfather had kept tied to the dock of his cottage in Puerto Rico. Ben, plunged into a state of absolute despondency, couldn't even bring himself to ask for silence.

The script had failed at the first fold.

It drove him crazy that he could see no fundamental shift in the nature of the code. Whatever Villaseñor had done to escalate the difficulty of the encryption, he had obscured it successfully. And he had done so not knowing that Ben had successfully cracked the early iterations of the encryption.

Kiral took one look at his face as he came through the door and understood all. She placed her hand on Amina's lower back, and Amina, who was at the stove, turned her head with a smile, not yet aware of the bad news. Kiral's expression said it all, and Amina nodded once, exchanged another significant glance with Kiral, and turned back to the stove.

Ben passed Alejandrx coming out of the bathroom, too ashamed even to raise his eyes. Shx let him pass.

He showered and changed, all the while wracking his mind for a solution. He could assume no more flashes of insight. No more secret allegories from an old history.

Of course Villaseñor had deepened the decryption. His entire sinecure was at stake. It was always risky to have put the early dot knot code out into the world. Arrogant, hubristic, condescending, yes—but risky. His rivals, Ben among them, would not have announced their successes to the world.

There was a knock at the bathroom door, and Ben was jarred from his machinations. When he emerged, he found Alejandrx waiting for him.

—The food is ready.

Ben nodded.

To his surprise, shx took his hand in hxrs and squeezed.

—I believe you can do this. Eat. Sleep. There is time.

"Not enough."

Shx nodded. —There is very little we can control.

A strange notion. His class, his clan, thrived on control. Control of circumstance, control of breeding, control of technology, bureaucracy, diet, training, education.

And yet.

Here he was, at the mercy of a social contrivance, the ritual of the convocation of the clans, the authority of the clan-sword. As if his ancestors had not established such rituals precisely to insulate his lineage from circumstance.

It was a troubling thought and he shook it off. And besides, it wasn't about that anymore. It was personal. He was determined to crack the new encryption. If he could not do it, then he was a fraud, and he did not deserve to ascend.

Amina sat tonight beside Kiral, their small affections now unhidden in the passing about of dishes, ladles, wine. Mobo, whom Ben had not seen in days, was there, sleepy-eyed and sullenly nursing a beer.

To Ben's delight, Alejandrx sat beside him, and because he was still spinning away in the slush of his mind, shx had the good grace to serve him from the communal bowls that made their way around the table.

The food smelled wonderful, sharp and piquant, and with a bite or two to whet his palette, Ben was able to eat hungrily. He noticed then that there remained an empty chair.

As if by destiny, the front door swung open at that moment and Dmitri Madrid came hurtling through the doorway, not bothering to divest himself of his vast charcoal overcoat. He crossed the apartment in three strides and set down upon the table before Ben a bundle draped in black cloth.

Ben, rattled, bent his neck up at the enormous Madrid, who was beaming under his grey mustache.

"Best work of my fucking life, Nakamura!"

Ben reached gingerly for the black bundle, unfolded the outer wrapping to reveal the Nakamura Matsukata.

He could not believe it. He took up the sword in both hands, ran his fingers along the saya, counting the braids of the ito.

The attention to detail was exquisite. The tsuka was inlaid with jade and pearl.

"How in God's name…"

Ben couldn't conceal his admiration.

Madrid laughed. "We're talking about the most famous sword in the world, lad. Every detail's been catalogued. What you're holding there's a rival to Matsukata himself."

Ben scowled.

"Don't fret, my boy. A well-trained eye will quickly spot the tell."

For a moment Ben was confused. Then, to confirm his suspicions, he drew from the scabbard a few inches of the blade. There, just above the hilt guard, was a tiny etching:

マドリッド

Madoriddo. Ben ran his finger over the etching. It was clever, damn him.

"Careful, lad," Madrid said. "It'll take your finger clean off."

Ben slid the blade back into its scabbard.

Madrid draped his enormous coat over the back of the open chair, then drew a couple of bottles of beer from the fridge. He handed one over to Mobo, who accepted in the spirit of companionship. Then he sank into his seat and began to eat.

AFTER THE MEAL, when the others had begun to clear the table, Kiral came to collect the sword. Ben held it for just a moment longer.

"It feels so real."

"Dmitri's work is extraordinary," she said. "You understand why I cannot let you have the replica."

Ben nodded. It didn't matter how real this one appeared to be. Were he to present it at the convocation of the clans, he would be setting himself up for Villaseñor's check mate.

"Who will wear the sword?"

Kiral didn't understand.

"Who will wear the sword when we go to retrieve the Matsukata?"

"Whom do you think?"

"I just wanted to make sure."

He handed the sword, enveloped once more, to Kiral, who held it cradled in the crook of her arm like a baby.

"I take it the advances in the dot knot technology are proving difficult."

Ben glanced around. The others appeared to be absorbed in the details of wiping down the table, boiling water for coffee. Amina, ever perceptive, came over to where they were standing, a dish towel over her shoulder, leaving a dark spot on the front of her yellow blouse.

"What do you need, Mr. Nakamura?"

"Access to the internet."

Amina frowned. "That's impossible."

"Barring that, I need resources. Books."

"Of course. One moment. Patrick?"

Hong glanced up from where he was about to sit down to a cup of tea.

"Hong can acquire even very rare texts."

Hong perked up. "You need books? What kind of books?"

Ben wracked his mind. "Books on ciphers. Code breaking. The mathematics of...folding? Origami! Books on origami."

Of course. The folds in the original dot knot had followed regular patterns, not unlike what would emerge from the origami folding of a geometric plane. If that was the basic underlying idea, then likely Villaseñor was only engaged in more complex geometric folding, shapes which perhaps were irregular, but discoverable.

Ben was almost relieved. He could barely hear Hong's nattering on about the details and assurances.

"There is one more thing."

"What?"

"Who told you how to fold the Descartes floor?"

EIGHTEEN

BEN AWOKE TO find a stack of books on the round table and a woman seated in one of the armchairs, legs crossed, idly smoking a cigarette, which could only have been procured on the black market. She was old and thin, with long white hair pinned up at the back of her head in a tight bun. She wore a robe-like black sweater that fell nearly to her ankles, and her wrists were thick with silver bangles. Her toenails, in open-toed black high heels, were cherry red.

"Who are you?"

"I am Irina Moiseyev," she said. Her accent was thick. "What is your problem?"

"Beg pardon?"

"I am Amina's geometrician. You need mathematics. So, I come."

"Oh. Yes." Ben scanned for his laptop. It was there among the books. "I can show you."

"No. Tell me. I don't like computer."

So Ben told her.

"You wish to calculate the shape from the, how you said—folds of the plane."

"Yes. Earlier versions of the code followed fairly straightforward rules for shapes like the Platonic solids. And in theory my algorithm can teach itself to test for different patterns, based on my input parameters. All that being said, I'm stuck."

"But we have books. So." She took a final drag on her cigarette. "We read."

Ben handed her a sampling of the books. Irina surveyed the titles, drew out a red-bound volume called *The Mathematical Precepts of Origami*, and began to read.

BEN DID NOT know what to expect, but sitting and waiting as Irina read for several hours was not it.

He flipped through some of the more accessible books, drawn in by the incredible complexity of the origami illustrations. Almost as beautiful were the diagrams of the underlying crease patterns, which, Ben read, could be discerned upon unfolding the shape *or* calculated mathematically with the goal of folding a particular shape.

"I suppose what we're looking for is some way to recover the crease pattern," he said aloud.

"That is proper deduction."

Ben went to pour himself a cup of tea. Irina looked up from her book.

"I have question."

"Yes?" He chose a bag of rooibos, acrid and pungent.

"How many folds in the old code?"

"Thousands."

Irina's eyes lit up. "In one place?"

"I misunderstood. At a given junction, perhaps two or three. Why?"

"There is upper bound to how many times you can fold a paper. Derives from ratio of length of the sheet to thickness of paper. Fold too much, paper is thicker than wide and bam! Limit. This—" she shook the page she was on, "is folding seven times. Thinner papers, maybe one, two more times."

"I'm not following."

"You are doing folds on computer, yes? Is not paper. Is not even plane. So, why is there limit to folds at a given juncture."

Ben sighed.

"You are unconvinced."

"No. It's the opposite. I know the man who designed the puzzle. You've intuited precisely the way that he would exploit the…"

Ben's voice trailed off.

It wouldn't be about the number of folds. His algorithm hadn't established a limit on the number of folds to explore at each juncture. If it were as simple as that, it would be rendered a computational error—time-consuming as hell, but not prone to kicking back the category errors he was seeing in the new script runs.

"You are having—"

"Wait." Ben raised a hand. Irina, bemused, struck a match and lit another cigarette.

"You're absolutely right. The plane is a contrivance. I'd had the thought and lost it—the code space could easily take place in three dimensions. Not four, because the code is static in time. But three, yes. I've been scanning for squares when what I'm looking for is cubes."

Irina was nodding. "Why only three? Again, is not plane."

"I don't…"

"There are mathematics of many dimensions."

"Why wasn't I seeing them?"

"Perhaps you are not knowing how to look. Not with your—" she shook her hand violently at the laptop there on the table. "—machine."

What would it mean for the code to exist in multiple dimensions? Was it a matter of telling it to perform a different kind of calculation? Could the algorithm do the calculations quickly enough to perform a multi-dimensional read and decrypt?

"I can imagine a three-dimensional space. I'm struggling as it is to imagine the code occupying such a space. Beyond three—it seems impossible."

"I'm permitted to make recommendation?"

"Of course."

"Don't imagine. Compute."

AND COMPUTE, SHE did.

The early dot knots were written so that having unfolded the code, you discovered a simple calculation at its heart, a proverbial hoop where solving correctly for X returned a set of instructions in the encryption telling it to disengage. Properly unfolding the dot knot was the lion's share of the computational work, and that could only be done if the read program was accurate. So, Irina spent her days working through the mathematics of multi-dimensional space, while Ben did his best to turn her calculations into instructions for the read-and-decrypt.

He was working in her domain on her terms, and he was exhausted. The creeping steps they made to translate her calculations into instructions for the algorithm were indisputably the most difficult he had ever undertaken.

And the computing power of the device Amina had given him gnawed at him. If she could get the math to work, and he could get it into code...the computing still needed to get done. So, during the long hours that Irina worked alone on the math, Ben refined his code, striving for the parsimoniousness of a Zen koan.

THEN THEY WERE done.

Irina stood behind him, staring at Ben's screen with barely concealed disdain.

"This is the...result?"

The lines of the algorithm were laid out in nested computational formulae, bracketed and staggered like the steps of a sine curved Ziggurat.

"That's the decrypt, yes."

"Ah." She walked away.

"What now?"

Ben had told Kiral the night before that they were getting close. She had remained behind that day in quiet expectation. "Are you ready to test it?"

She proffered the drive that contained the latest dot knot.

"And if is wrong?" Irina poured herself a cup of black coffee.

Ben massaged the bridge of his nose. "If the code is wrong, it will return an error and I'll have to troubleshoot the syntax."

"I mean for whole thing. Is much work for nothing."

Ben turned to Kiral. As if she would know.

She did not answer aloud. Instead she spoke by sign.

—What happens to a dream deferred?

Ben plugged in the drive.

NINETEEN

BEN WOKE WITH the first light. He went into the kitchen, where Mobo, dressed in his yellow work jumpsuit, sat sipping tea and eating from a plate of fried yams and moi moi with pap. He gestured to a platter of hot food at the center of the table.

"Is Amina here?" He assumed that she had cooked. He'd never seen Mobo do more than rummage for a bottle opener.

"Shower."

"Kiral?"

Mobo's eyes narrowed slightly. "She is also in the shower."

He took a bite of the blended bean roll, stared at Ben as he fixed himself a cup of coffee.

"Tomorrow is the job, yeah?"

Ben nodded.

"So, you get your special sword back, then what?"

"I replace my father as titular head of the clan."

"Because of the sword?"

"Something like that."

"They know you lose it?"

Ben didn't respond.

"You trust my sister?"

Ben was surprised to detect a note of dissonance in Mobo's tone. "Should I not?"

"You paying good money? Yeah? She'll do the job good for you."

"Why does she want the money?"

"Why we all want money? She got plans for it."

"What plans?"

Mobo rooted in the corner of his mouth with his tongue, shrugged deep. He went dim behind the eyes.

"Aren't you part of this?"

"For me, she is my sister. I help her out. I get a little money. My sister's plans, I don't know nothing about them."

"What plans?" Kiral came in from the hallway, tucking the last strands of her hair into her hijab, fawn-colored over a white shirt and blue jeans.

Mobo rose and took his plate to the sink. He left it and zipped up his jumpsuit. He didn't say anything else to either of them, hardly glanced back on his way out the door.

Amina came in from the hall a moment later. Ben watched as Kiral met her eyes. They seemed to speak without words, either telepathically or through experience.

Amina came and sat at the table with Ben. Kiral went to the kitchen to make tea. To his relief, she did not condescend by pretending that her brother should be dismissed.

"My brother and I do not always see eye to eye, Mr. Nakamura. That has nothing to do with you."

Ben nodded.

"For you, the recovery of the sword is existential. For me, it is a job."

"That's what your brother said. About himself."

Amina laughed.

"I wonder whether we mean the same thing. I have

distance from the stakes. I can approach the problem of the theft analytically. I can promise you, Ben, on my word, that forty-eight hours from now, you will have the sword. After all, I do want your money."

"Your brother said that too."

"Then you know I am not lying."

"Why do you want it? The sum is considerable."

"I want it for the same reasons you do, Mr. Nakamura."

"Power." He may once have believed it, but he found now that its truth rang hollow.

Amina shook her head.

"Not power. Freedom. What we want is freedom."

"What is freedom?"

Amina rose abruptly from the table.

"Finish your meal. We have a busy day."

Reina caught him as they came into the warehouse. Beyond her, Hong and Dmitri were arguing about football as they rolled the Descartes Room out to the center of the warehouse. Ben owned one of the teams. Apparently, Hong was a fan, while Madrid preferred the style of play among the Old European variation of the sport. Ben cared little for team sports, and so paid them little mind.

"You got the laptop?"

Ben nodded.

Reina led him to the downstairs office. He burst out laughing when he saw what it was. Not an office, but a living room, complete with a couch, recliners, bookshelves and a table in the corner. There was a box on the table, and it was to this box that Reina led him.

"Amina said you did the thing?"

Ben breathed deep and nodded. Yes. He had done the thing.

He and Irina. He felt a small pang at her absence. He was not sure what to call the tie that bound them. They had accomplished something truly groundbreaking together, and in an extraordinarily brief, intense time. They had worked well together. He did not know who she was, but he felt that he knew her. If they recovered the sword—when—he would try to find her again. She could come to work for him, perhaps.

No, never for him. With him.

Of course that was absurd.

It was the first time he acknowledged to himself that this strange, liminal period would come to an end. There was relief in the thought, but also sadness. There was something special about being among these people. He would have to be a fool not to see it. It was so strange, so new, that he found he could not name it. It was unlike anything he had ever known.

Deeper than the sadness was something else. Something uncomfortable, raw. Pain.

He had not seen Alejandrx all week, and the compulsive thought that shx was not there that morning because shx would not ever be there again made his heart ache, though he knew it not to be true.

Reina removed two parcels from the box. She held up first one, then the other.

"This is what you're going to put your computer thing in. *This* is something new. It's a transponder. After you do the first thing, you click in the second thing. That's gonna let us watch you from the inside."

Ben nodded.

"How long it's gonna take you to do the computer?"

"I don't know. Half an hour. That's if it all goes well."

"Do it quick. Your suit's upstairs. Kiral said she has news."

twenty

They had drilled the run only twice that day. Ben suspected that Amina wanted them to reserve their strength for the following night.

Instead, they packed everything they would need. Kiral and Madrid were going ahead to ensure that the tech would work. Ben had asked once or twice where exactly that was, but he had been politely rebuffed.

Reina, after his third attempt, had been less polite: "You're on a need-to-know basis. Do you need to know?"

Ben conceded that he didn't. Reina made a face like she'd been skunked. "Then why the hell you keep asking?"

Ben kept his composure. They were all exhausted, and with the job tomorrow, every nerve was frayed.

After Kiral and Madrid were gone, Alejandrx asked to speak to Amina privately. They disappeared together into the downstairs room.

Hong caught Ben's eye and asked for help covering the Descartes Room with the tarp. By the time that was finished, Reina too was gone. Hong left unceremoniously not long afterwards.

Unsure whether Amina or Alejandrx would be his chaperone back to the apartment, Ben waited. They were in there for so long that he began to wonder whether they too had gone, and he was waiting there for orders that would never come.

He was debating whether to go over and knock on the door—they might just be making conversation—when the door opened, and they came out. Alejandrx saw him, turned to Amina and signed something that Ben could not see. Amina turned her gaze to where he stood, her face impassive. She took a moment to respond, but she took Alejandrx's hand and gave it a squeeze.

For a split second his heart clenched—could they too be entangled?—but Alejandrx dipped hxr shoulder, spun on one toe and came directly over to him. Ben's heart leapt. He had hoped that it was shx who would take him back.

—I want to show you something.

"I haven't showered."

—It's not important. Come.

Shx extended a hand. He took it and they left the warehouse hand in hand.

Until then, he had always been transported to and from the warehouse by VTOL. Now, Alejandrx went to a corner of the lot, stopping before a burlap tarp. Shx flung the tarp back to reveal a glistening black hoverbike with silver trim. Ben set his fingertips on the rear seat. This was an expensive machine. And he still had no idea how Alejandrx made a living.

Shx pressed the ignition and the bike hummed to life, rising from the perch of its retractable tripod, a thrust of air kicking up a tiny tsunami of dust and paper scraps, giving the air around them the prickle of an electric charge.

Alejandrx unclasped a lever in the seat, which sprang open. Shx withdrew two helmets.

—You first.

Ben pulled the helmet on and threw his leg over the bike. He gripped the handlebars and scanned the iridescent red dash to acquaint himself with the readouts, which were now displayed on the inner visor.

He turned back to Alejandrx, who gave hxr head the slightest cock.

—At the back.

Ben flushed. Of course. He pushed himself backwards onto the rear seat as gracefully as he could, the dash projection disabling itself as he left its range. Alejandrx took the driver's seat. Then, shx reached back and took his hands, wrapping them snugly around hxr waist.

—Tighter, shx commanded. He obeyed.

They moved slowly as shx maneuvered out of the lot, before blasting incomprehensibly fast down the derelict stretch of the old avenue, through the narrow gullet of an alley and into the steady flow of electric bus traffic.

Ben cried out at the sudden burst of speed, and as if to further embarrass him, Alejandrx accelerated. Ben tightened his grip around hxr waist. Shx slipped into the space of his body. He could feel the power in hxr back, hxr stomach, hxr thighs.

Alejandrx carved a twisting route through the outerborough grid, the hoverbike moving like a mako shark on the scent of mackerel. Ben was immediately and irretrievably lost. They moved quickly from the post-industrial outskirts of Red Hook to avenues lined with blue-glassed high rise apartments, and finally onto the pock-marked corridor of the BQE.

At last, shx pulled off the highway into a neighborhood of low brick shops and restaurants and bodegas, over which had been erected several generations of varying architecture.

Alejandrx turned the bike into another capillary alleyway. Shx threaded past towers of wooden palettes, tires, and empty plastic buckets with decals in Mandarin, Amharic and Greek. At the end of the alley there was a cracked concrete courtyard. Half a dozen bicycles leaned against the back of a single-story whitewashed building.

Alejandrx cut the engine and the hoverbike settled slowly onto its tripod. Shx squeezed his hands. Ben unclasped and descended, wobbly-kneed. He drew off his helmet and allowed the mellow dusk breeze to cool him.

Alejandrx ran a hand through hxr hair. There was a tattoo at the nape of hxr neck which he had never noticed, a sharp black sigil of Mercury.

"Where are we?"

Alejandrx indicated a battered red door, over which had been affixed a sign: *Kendo Kweens*.

Ben brightened. Between the runs and the drills in the warehouse, he had kept fit, and he had gotten into the habit of ending his evenings in the apartment with some light calisthenics and yoga to stay limber. Still, he missed the ritual of his kendo training, the weight of a sword in his hands, the feel of wood underfoot. Alejandrx had understood that he felt its lack.

Once, the dojo might have been beautiful. It was shabby now, the walls lined with cheap wooden racks stocked with equipment. Someone had hand-painted the Japanese names for each piece—*shinai*, *bogu*—on cream-colored paper above each rack.

Half a dozen practitioners were already there, dressed in full kendōgu.

One man, lean and Black, his wire men tucked under his arm, turned from where he was observing a pair of students. His eyes flicked from Benjiro to Alejandrx and back. He cocked an eyebrow, then grinned.

"Finally, some competition, Ale, yeah?" His accent was thick.

There were a few nods of recognition now from the other kendōka. Several turned and bowed. Ben reciprocated. He had wondered whether he would be recognized.

—We share our equipment.

It was a statement of fact, unapologetic. Shx knew he could buy this dojo a hundred million times over.

The changing room was discrete. There was a low bench along a mirrored wall, and a bamboo shelf for storing his clothes. Ben dressed in the keikogi and hakama Alejandrx had found for him. They fit well enough, and were, at least, laundered. He stared at himself for a moment in the mirror. He was haggard, lean, unkempt. Rugged.

Strong.

The final step was to wrap his head in a black cotton tenugui. His hands followed the familiar motion.

The armor would be waiting in the dojo.

Alejandrx too was waiting for him, the owner helping hxr into hxr bogu. All that remained was to fit the men over hxr tenugui.

When shx was attired, Ben had his turn and in a few minutes they were ready. They had already selected their swords, having elected to train with bokken, katana-shaped swords carved from a single piece of wood. They were well-made, sturdy. None had the balance Ben was used to, but this was to be expected. He wondered off-handedly whether any of the other kendōka even perceived the imperfections.

Alejandrx picked one at random.

They faced one another now on the wooden sprung floor. Ben shifted his weight from foot to foot. The grip was good.

He wondered which of them would initiate shikake-waza, which would parry with ōji-waza.

They had interrupted a fairly advanced lesson. In deference to his status, both as a guest and as a master swordsman, the earlier practitioners had stepped aside to watch their local excellence challenge the Olympian.

They had removed their helmets, and the woman, he was surprised to see, wore her hair in a headscarf. Her companion was shorter, broad across the chest, brown-skinned, probably Filipino.

Benjiro figured he would give them a show.

Never in his decades of training, never in the years spent medaling at the highest echelons of elite competition, had he come up against an opponent like Alejandrx. It did not take him long to see that it was he who was being played with.

Shx moved with the precision of a cheetah, the lightning lethality of a striking scorpion. Hxr calls, despite hxr deafness, were crisp and clear and rattling, and shx seemed to know his mind before he struck. There was an effortlessness to hxr swordsmanship that Benjiro could not even dare to envy.

He did not know how long shx had trained. It did not matter. This was more than training, more than diligence. Shx had a gift unlike anything he had ever seen, wielding hxr botuko as if it were an extension of hxr very soul. Ben knew he was in the presence of a transcendent master, and his heart was glad.

Shx was not gifted.

No.

Shx was a gift.

Afterwards, when they were heading back to the hoverbike, shx asked him only if he was hungry. Already his muscles ached with the strain of trying to keep up with hxr.

In this strange new humility, Ben could only laugh.

"Yes. Quite."

—Good. I know a place.

Shx took him deeper north and west into Queensborough. Traffic thinned considerably, and Alejandrx slowed the bike so as not to hit any of the multitudes who wandered into the otherwise abandoned roadway; they were as likely now to see a flock of feral hens.

This time, shx parked street-side. A handful of kids approached them sidelong. Alejandrx took a wad of bills from hxr pocket, stripped a few to hand to the oldest kid, dark-haired, like Ben, his hair pulled back into a topknot. He wore a bright yellow jacket over dark jeans. His shoes were so white they glowed.

"Keep it safe."

Shx said this aloud, in the monotone of hxr spoken voice.

"Yeah, alright."

Ben was confused. Valet parking in the outerboroughs? But Alejandrx took his hand and led him into a restaurant. A bell tinkled as they pushed open the door.

It was tidy and cramped with round Formica tables. The walls were mostly bare, save for a few spots where cramped picture frames held photographs of landscapes that could hold meaning only to an initiate.

No one gave Benjiro and Alejandrx more than a cursory glance.

They found a two-top by the window looking out over the street. Though it was late, the streets were quickly filling with people. There must be a public hospital nearby, for an exodus of nurses marked the turnover of shifts. A handful of them came inside to order takeout from a brusque old woman behind the counter.

Ben was so lost in the people-watching that he was startled to hear Alejandrx speaking in rapid Spanish. A pretty waitress, brown-skinned, with long shiny black hair, stood beside them, carefully setting bottles of beer and tall glasses of ice between them.

"What's this?" There was a bright red slurry at the bottom of each glass. Alejandrx ignored the question until shx had poured half a beer into each glass.

—It's a michelada. You'll like it.

She spelled *michelada* so that he could understand.

Ben sipped the strange concoction. It was pleasantly spicy, the heat of the chili sauce undercut by the coolness of the beer. They took a few sips and Alejandrx topped them off from the other beer.

Shx seemed as content as he with the silence between them. He had a thousand questions for hxr, but none felt as urgent as they had two weeks ago. For now, he was happy only to take hxr in.

Hxr hair was curlier than he had first noticed. Shx kept it so short, it was hard to spot. But now, sweaty from the dojo and the hoverbike helmet, the ends lay in thick wet curls against hxr forehead.

Shx had slipped off hxr leather jacket and was wearing a tight long-sleeved white t-shirt under a baggy black tank top, the sleeves pushed up to the elbows. It was, he realized, the first time he had noticed hxr bare arms were covered in tattoos. On her left forearm unfurled twin flags, their staffs crossed, one red, one black. On the other was the flag of Honduras, two bands of blue flanking a white stripe, five blue stars.

There were geometric symbols, too: a circle whose circumference was coterminous with the vertices of a square, into which was set an isosceles triangle.

Ben indicated the geometry. "What does that mean?"

Alejandrx laughed.

—In my country, I studied to be...how do you say *botánico*?

"A botanist?"

Shx nodded. —Is a symbol from botany.

"When did you come here?"

—I came here to live with my aunt and her wife when I was–

The dark-haired waitress reappeared with two long white platters, which she set in the center of the table. Next to this she placed a wire rack with an assortment of brightly colored sauces in stoppered glass bottles.

"Buen provecho." The waitress withdrew.

On the plates, propped upright by a slotted wire rack were thick, beautifully browned cornmeal tacos wrapped in wax paper and stuffed to overflowing.

"It smells amazing."

—They are arepas. Traditional in my country.

"What's in them?"

—It's many different things. Beans and white cheese. Chicken with avocado. Pork with chilies, and—

Shx could see that something was wrong.

—What?

Ben had been raised vegan. It was a fact of his caste which, until that moment, had never been troubled. All the cooking at the apartment had been vegan, or vegetarian, and Ben had assumed that it was a fact of life for Amina and her crew as well.

He wondered whether there were a challenge in it: was shx daring him to eat or to forgo?

"I thought you were vegetarian."

—No. Kiral is, so Amina asks us to honor her wishes when we dine together so that we are not, how you say, unincluded at her table.

Ben did his best to smile. Alejandrx had not yet reached for an arepa. Shx was waiting for him, as hxr guest. Ben invoked the memory of Alcibiades, and resolved to throw himself into the moment.

He reached for the black bean and white cheese. He was not sure of the etiquette for consuming it. He glanced around the restaurant to see whether there were anyone else he could mimic.

Alejandrx solved the dilemma for him, reaching for the chicken arepa and then drizzling it in a bright green sauce.

"What are the sauces?"

—They are spicy.

"I enjoy spicy food."

—This is guasacaca. From Venezuela. Still, it is good.

Ben drizzled his arepa and took a bite.

It was a revelation. He found himself setting the arepa down on his plate to stare at it in contemplation.

Alejandrx watched him, curiosity mixed with anxiety.

—Do you like it?

"It's amazing. It's really quite amazing."

—Good. Then you can pay for it.

Shx fumbled in the pocket of her leather jacket, which hung on hxr seat back, and withdrew his wallet, watch and phone. Shx slid them across the table, depositing them beside his plate. He reached for them, and his fingers brushed hxr knuckles. He froze, not wanting to seem forward, but not wanting to move. Shx let his hand rest there, and then, after a moment, turned hxr hand palm up, so that their fingers could interlace.

To Ben's surprise, shx blushed.

—It is difficult to eat arepas with one hand.

So shx found his leg with hxr foot, and they interlocked their ankles, each adjusting, laughing at the strangeness, the pleasant discomfort, and the expectation that caused the blood to run hotter in their veins.

Ben had longed for his phone, for contact with his staff, his family. He found now that the thought of turning it on and seeing their desperate messages was dreadful to him.

His appetite and hxr touch proved more than sufficient incentive to leave the damned thing be. He devoured what remained of his arepa and turned next to the chicken and avocado.

After a few hungry minutes of pleasant and playful gorging, they leaned back in their chairs and drained their micheladas.

"Do you want another?" He was paying, after all.

—Not yet. I don't want to drive...

Shx raised a hand and tilted it back and forth.

Ben nodded. The alcohol, little as it was, had already gone to his head.

Alejandrx signaled for the check, and when it came, Ben reached for his wallet. He withdrew a credit card but paused.

"If I pay—"

He didn't need to finish the thought. His family had by now undoubtedly contacted the banks to put a trace on his cards. Of course, he didn't carry cash.

—Is no problem.

"Thank you."

Shx smiled.

—Something small from my country.

There was a note of longing in hxr expression.

Alejandrx dug in hxr pocket for the wad of bills. Shx lay a few down in a tidy stack under the corner of her plate. Ben glanced around—would no one try to snag the cash as they left? But no one seemed to notice their departure.

It was the same with the boys who watched the bike. At their emergence from the restaurant, one of the boys materialized, accepted another stack of bills, and then retreated.

"How do they decide which of them will keep the money?"

Alejandrx looked confused.

—Who?

"The boys. Why does that one get to keep the money?"

—But he will disburse it among his companions.

"Why? Why not keep it for himself?"

Hxr expression softened from confusion to something akin to delight. Shx was enjoying his indoctrination.

—Because one day he will not be the lucky one.

Shx pulled the leather jacket on and handed him a helmet.

"Where to next?"

Would shx take him back to the apartment?

—Home.

FOR A LONG time after, Ben lay awake, his arm across Alejandrx's back while shx slept, hxr head pressed hard into the space between his pectoral muscle and the curve of his jaw.

Hxr quarters were small, bare bones, utterly devoid of aesthetic. There was something provisional about it, utilitarian. A chin up bar clung to the doorframe between the living room, where they lay on a fold-out bed, and the kitchenette. In the corner was a collapsible closet, hung with a handful of things. There was a green yoga mat in the corner, and a pair of cactuses in ceramic pots in the window.

Alejandrx stirred, ran a finger through the hair on his chest. Ben kissed hxr forehead. He was unused to tenderness and the instinctiveness of it unsettled him. It seemed to surprise Alejandrx too. Shx pushed hxrself up so that shx was seated and stretched so that every fiber of hxr musculature could be seen. Ben, unable to stop himself, put his hand against hxr stomach.

It was the first time he saw the jagged scars that crisscrossed hxr abdomen, chest and thighs.

If shx saw him notice them, shx did not betray it. Instead, shx rose and went into the kitchenette, not bothering to put anything on. Ben lay back and watched hxr. Shx was utterly unselfconscious.

Shx started water for coffee, then came back to stand in the doorway.

"How do you want your coffee?"

"Black."

Shx turned back to the kitchenette. Then, as if having a second thought, shx rose to hxr tiptoes and took hold of the chin up bar. Shx did twenty chin ups the way any ordinary person might warm up by jogging in place. Turning hxrself to face him, shx raised hxr legs so that shx was bent nearly in half. She raised and lowered hxrself another twenty times, then spread hxr legs into the splits. Slow as molasses, shx lowered hxr legs, still splayed, until all at once shx let go the bar and dropped silently to hxr feet.

"You're incredible."

Shx turned away from him so that he could not see hxr expression and went to retrieve the kettle, which had begun to rattle. Shx came back to the bed with clay mugs and a French press of fragrant coffee. Shx sank to hxr knees on the bed and handed Ben a mug. She set the press to steep beside the bed.

"I have so many questions."

—I will answer what I can.

"How did you defeat me? Yesterday, in kendo. I'm no amateur, but I would be embarrassed if I were not in awe."

The question surprised hxr. Perhaps shx had assumed he would ask about the scars, hxr body, hxr history, the team.

—You were fighting to show off.

Ben smiled. "A little, yes. Modesty has never been my strong suit."

Alejandrx took his cup and, setting both aside, put hxr hands on his hips and swung hxrself into his lap. Shx took his long hair in hxr fingers and pressed hxr mouth against his.

They moved to come together. When he was inside hxr, shx bent hxr head to his ear.

"I was afraid you would forget me."

twenty one

THE MOON WAS high, bright. The only sound was the lapping of the river against the boggy bank where they had squatted, awaiting the night.

Ben's insides were knotted. His only consolation was the press of Alejandrx's hand against his, the way hxr fingers stroked the back of his hand from time to time.

All at once there was a change in the air, the sound of a boat's motor drawing closer. Amina rose and tapped her wrist. For a split second the time glowed green.

"Move quickly."

Alejandrx nodded.

With a practiced tug, shx drew down hxr hood. In the near darkness the glassy red eyes seemed almost black. Shx fixed the spider-like breathing apparatus to hxr mouth. Ben did the same.

—Fit me with the sword.

Amina looped the scabbard across hxr back, cinched the crosswise strap tight.

The replica sword secured, Amina too now drew on her mask. Her eyes shone green. It was a convention they had followed long before the contract with Ben. In the blackness of night, sealed up in the bug suits, the faintest shimmer of color could help them to distinguish one another.

Amina and Ben climbed into a rubber dinghy they had inflated that afternoon. Ben held the ultra-lightweight oars steady while Alejandrx pushed off from the marshy bank of the Old Fort Totten reserve. Shx slipped into the stern and began to row, moving them quickly into the center of the East River, where they caught the current and began to pick up speed. All the while the engine sound grew louder, thrumming the air, until it seemed it was the only sound in the world.

Ben turned and saw a vast barge bearing down on them, fast-moving, inexorable. Alejandrx cut the water hard to slice the angle of their approach. Amina was halfway up the rope ladder that hung over its side before Ben realized what they were doing. He rose, rocking the dinghy and nearly capsizing it. Alejandrx raised an oar to prop the dinghy upright.

"Come!" Amina hissed.

Ben caught the ladder in shaking hands and began to climb. Alejandrx tossed the oars into the bottom of the dinghy and ascended behind him, giving the dinghy a rough push with one foot as shx pulled away.

Amina had crept over to the pilot's house. Ben followed on his hands and knees. The smell was nauseating. Of course, Reina would send a garbage barge.

They leaned against the door to the pilot's house, Ben exhorting himself not to vomit in the bug suit. Alejandrx came up beside them.

—How long is the boat ride?

They had told him almost nothing about this part

of the plan. It was not need-to-know. Instinctively, he squeezed the pocket on his utility belt that contained the dot knot decrypting tech. Still there.

To Ben's surprise, it was not Amina or Alejandrx who answered. The text came in orange.

—Speeds top out at 5 knots around some of the islands.

—That's not what I asked and I don't know what that means.

—Thirty minutes, give or take.

This time it was Amina.

—This is some boat.

—Excuse me?

—It was supposed to be a joke.

—I see. Listen carefully.

A strange turn of phrase, given the circumstances. The orange letters came quickly:

—The barge is going to dock to the sea wall. Normally, that sends a signal to the dumpsters to come over and tip out their loads. Mobo has set it so that the barge will flood the receiver, causing a local electrical crash. The system will attempt to reboot for six cycles. Between each cycle we have thirty seconds. After the sixth cycle, the system generates a fail-safe and the rest of the consulate will go on red alert. That means we have six windows to make the climb.

—Two a person.

He was sure shx meant it as an assurance, but the words rankled. It really meant he had four tries.

—And if we miss the windows?

—The barge will decouple and toggle a signal for the next one to finish what it would not.

—And what will happen to this one?

—She will follow the current out to sea.

THEY DID NOT speak again. There was nothing else to say. A small part of him wished that he could sit with Alejandrx, entangle himself with hxr, draw comfort from hxr touch. Shx remained at a remove, crouched on hxr haunches, hxr head turned to the Manahatta shoreline, alert. The horrible rumbling of the barge's engines must be rather a different experience for hxr.

A lump rose in Ben's throat. He did not know how he would see hxr again, after this. He only knew that he desired it with all his heart. That there were mere hours left—he pushed the thought from his mind.

Yet it returned to him.

He had never allowed the word love into his vision of the future. When he married, it would be to a daughter of one of the other clans. The marriage would be primarily designed to consolidate power and defuse tension. She would be beautiful, well-bred, intelligent. A life could be made that way; his parents had not been unhappy.

Ben had never worried about such a life because he had never before known someone extraordinary. Alejandrx made him feel like a fool, plain and simple. Shx was unrivaled.

There was an obstinacy building in him, an impertinence with the world he must fall back into when all of this was done. Alejandrx could never be a consort. Why not bring hxr into his world? Let the others batter away about propriety, heredity. His sisters would no doubt have children. It was only by some accident of biology that he had been born first, born male. A nephew or niece could be a proper scion.

He would be happy, for he would have hxr.

THE BARGE ENGINE softened and the vessel began to list towards Manahatta.

—Places, everyone.

Alejandrx rose and went to climb up onto the roof of the engine room. There was no pilot—the entire network of barges was run by satellite. Ben too rose, though he did not climb.

There was a sudden grinding noise as the docking mechanism extended from the front of the barge. Ben didn't know how, but the docking mechanism piloted the barge to the sea wall and slipped into a receiving port.

This triggered Mobo's electrical interference, and within moments it seemed everyone was in motion.

Alejandrx was already steadying hxrself with one hand against the sea wall. Amina scrambled up beside hxr. Ben followed. The barge rocked underfoot. He was suddenly glad they had drilled on the artificial boat.

Amina signed a question for Kiral:

—What's our timing?

Kiral responded immediately.

—It will take forty-five seconds for the initial signal fail. After that, it will stagger in 30-second intervals beginning in 2 minutes and will continue for 6 cycles.

—Tell us when to begin.

—Wait. Here, better.

Kiral dropped a countdown timer into their visual displays. It hovered for a moment before tracking to the upper right-hand corner of his vision. There were just a couple of seconds left on the override.

As soon as the timer hit zero, it turned over.

Thus began the longest two minutes of Ben's life.

He stared up at the lip of the sea wall. His stomach sank. It was easily a foot higher than they had drilled. His knees went weak.

They waited in absolute silence for the signal. When the timer finally turned over to the first 30-second interval, Alejandrx burst into action. Shx moved like shx was untethered by gravity, springing up to catch the lip of the sea wall, and pulling hxr legs up in the same motion. Shx stood for half a moment on the tips of hxr toes on the lip of the wall. From one of the pockets on hxr belt shx drew a coin, which she tossed onto the fence to be sure of Mobo's timing. Thus assured, shx scaled the fence the way a gecko scales a window. Shx propelled hxrself over the top and dropped daintily on the other side. The timer ticked off another six seconds, then turned over.

—That's one.

Ben's heart pounded. Thirty seconds was not a lot of time. With every drop of the digits, he heard Reina over the bullhorn in the warehouse, "Dead! Dead! Dead!"

And they had not rehearsed with 10,000 volts of electricity.

At the next break, Amina bent her knees and leapt, catching the lip of the sea wall, but only barely. Her feet scrabbled against the wet concrete, unable to find a foothold. Ben provided his hands for a boost, but Amina dropped instead back onto the barge beside him.

—What happened?!

Kiral's heart must be in her throat.

—My decision. No foothold, no time. I'll take the next one if Ben can give me a boost.

It was the first time she had used his name.

—Yes.

—Can you get up without one?

—Of course, he signed, though the weakness in his knees belied his confidence.

The thirty seconds ticked off, then another. Ben knelt and formed a platform with his interlaced fingers. Amina set a foot there and waited for zero.

She pushed with one foot and Ben rose with a grunt, their shared effort getting her high enough to pull herself up with one knee. She wasted no time scrambling up the fence. Unlike Alejandrx, she climbed halfway down the other side before dropping, leaving just two seconds on the clock. Ben was up. The countdown clock started at 30.

To his horror, he found he could not move. He bent his knees to launch himself, but when the timer ticked down the final seconds and opened the first window, the familiar fear overtook him: what if they were lying? What if this was how they planned to do him in? Run half as many fail cycles on the fence and let him fry. The sword, if they wanted it, could be theirs…

Alejandrx signed to him:

—Ben? Is everything alright?

Benjiro could not answer.

Alejandrx drew up beside the fence.

—We need you.

Ben tried to absorb the meaning of these words. Shx was right. They had entrusted him with the decryptor. He was being paranoid.

Another cycle timed out. Kiral began to ping him directly:

—Mr. Nakamura, you are running out of time. There are only two more cycles.

Ninety seconds between success and oblivion. He knew he needed to push through. Knew too that what terrified him was not really the fear of being lied to.

No, what he feared was something hidden so deep within him that he had not imagined it was there: He was afraid of his own success. To ascend to the headship of the clan, to rule the sinecure—it was an awesome, terrifying leap.

The fear, finally acknowledged, seemed now to exist outside him. He had the sudden urge to leap and climb, and bent his knees to make the jump.

—Just ten more seconds, Kiral said.

A shiver ran down his spine. If she hadn't reminded him, he would have leapt out of instinct.

He glanced up. Alejandrx was still standing just inside the fencing, peering down. Ben steeled himself, edged closer to the sea wall. The barge rocked under foot. His muscles knew this all by heart.

When the timer turned over, Alejandrx put a hand on the fence.

—I won't let go until you cross.

Ben leapt. He made the sea wall in a single leap, caught the slippery side with his toes and managed to get a hold. He pushed himself up over the edge and grabbed the fence with splayed fingers.

He ascended as quickly as ever he had, trying his best to unsee the timer counting down the seconds to his obliteration.

5…4…3…

He dropped, landed hard on his ankle. He rose, took a few tentative steps to be sure it was not broken.

Kiral: —Your heart rate really got up there! ;)

Amina signed, —Your ankle?

—I'm fine.

Alejandrx came to him. He could not imagine what shx must be thinking behind the mask. To his surprise, shx threw hxr arms around him, pressing hxr forehead against his.

He held hxr trembling body for a moment before shx pulled away.

On the screens a new countdown timer had turned over, this one set to thirty minutes.

He took a few ginger steps. Amina and Alejandrx watched him.

—I'm fine. Let's go.

It hurt like hell but he could push through it. His heart was still pounding, his ears ringing. Behind them the barge decoupled from the sea wall with an electric click. The engine roared back to life.

The worst of it, he told himself, was over.

twenty

THE CONSULATE CONSISTED of what had once been a block of townhouses on York Avenue. They had crossed the fence at the edge of a terraced green space that may once have been a public park. Now, it was a pleasant spot for the consulate staff to take their lunch.

The atrium was located at the far end of the consulate.

They had to ascend a low wall from the green space to a walkway that ran the length of the building.

They moved under cover of darkness. Mobo had arranged for the decoupling of the barge to set in motion a series of electrical failures, so that every security camera they approached would fail precisely long enough to trigger an automatic reboot, but not long enough to cause the system to read an error. If they moved quickly enough, accurately enough, they could pass invisibly between the outer fence and the atrium.

Ben fell in line between Amina and Alejandrx. Amina set a brisk pace, and they moved with practiced speed. Ben's mind was clear. The visceral feeling that had kept him motionless on the barge had washed out of his blood with the adrenaline.

Just ahead there was a narrow colonnade at the edge of a long sloping lawn. Ben had attended a handful of receptions and parties there over the years. The marble columns had been imported at considerable expense from the ruins of Ephesus. They were not to Ben's taste, but he admired the precocity.

Alejandrx took a running jump, got a lizard grip on the near-most column, and scaled quickly, pulling hxrself lithely up onto the pergola. There, shx crouched, already invisible in the darkness, save for the red glimmer of hxr bug eyes. Shx drew from hxr belt a rope, which Ben and Amina used to pull themselves up alongside hxr.

The pergola was a latticework of white wooden slats, gorgeously hung with climbing roses, wisteria, ruscus, honeysuckle and eucalyptus. Twin beams ran the length of the colonnade to the atrium, and it was along these beams that they scurried like alien mice.

From the far end of the colonnade, it was another few feet to ascend to the rooftop, and from there, a quick swing around to the northernmost face of the consulate, where the atrium had been appended to the building.

THE ATRIUM WAS a gorgeous Neo-Baroque construction of wrought steel and glass, and they crossed hand over foot towards its center, where a broad square opening had been left, an obscene lapse in judgement, and a testament to Villaseñor's love of birds.

Alejandrx unclasped from hxr belt a winch, which shx fastened to the steel rim of the opening. Shx handed the cable to Amina, who clipped herself to the carabiner and quickly descended the thirty or forty feet to the ground. When she unclasped, the winch spun the rope back up onto its axle with a neat snap.

First Ben, then Alejandrx followed. Shx, however, did not unclasp. Instead, shx gave two sharp tugs to the rope. It disconnected from the winch and streamed to the soft earth beside them. A moment later, the winch emitted a sharp click and rolled through the atrium's opening. Amina caught it and tossed it back to Alejandrx.

It was late enough that the roosting birds hardly fluttered at their sounds.

There was a security interface immediately beside the interior door, a strip of buttons under a hinged plastic shield. Never in a million years would Ben have seen it. Kiral alerted him to it by drawing a digital bead so that for a moment Ben could not even move his head until he signed his acknowledgment.

Kiral continued to send him instructions.

—Mobo says the port is on the underside.

Ben felt for it. There it was.

His heart began to pound. He drew the decryptor from his belt and connected through a three-foot stretch of fiber optic cable.

The decrypt engine ran on a vintage touch screen phone, which had been gutted and stuffed with as much computing power as it could physically handle.

Ben thumbed open the program file and connected to the security system interface. Prompted for a password, he typed in the instruction to run the code.

On the touchscreen an icon appeared, a stylized knot with a blood red pin in it, a gimmick Ben had written on a whim. He wanted to be able to say that he'd broken the dot knot as easily as pulling out the lynchpin.

He turned to Amina.

—Say when.

What happened next had been her idea. She drew from her belt a single firecracker, snapped it open, and tossed it into the center of the atrium. A second passed, then two. Then the firecracker exploded and every bird in the trees around them shot out of its branch, spiraling in a mad swirling cacophony towards the atrium's opening.

Ben tapped the icon.

For an interminable minute he waited, his hands shaking so hard he worried he would drop the decryptor. Alejandrx, beside him, took his hands.

Ben breathed. Waited. Breathed.

Then, under the roiling din of bird-cry and flapping wings, he heard the almost noiseless click of the lock disengaging.

We did it, Irina, Ben thought. Tears of relief in his eyes.

He disengaged the decryptor from the hard wire and handed it to Amina in exchange for what Reina had called *the other thing*.

He affixed this to the wire, then pulled gently on the spool to trigger the spring. The wire slipped noiselessly back into the case and the new device, far lighter than the decryptor, came to hang just below the security panel. Ben carefully flicked it on and waited for the tiny orange indicator light to stabilize.

—We're in, came the note from Kiral.

They slipped noiselessly through the door.

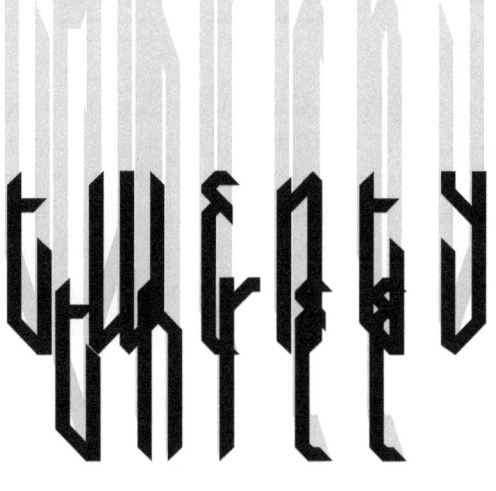

twenty

THEY MOVED QUICKLY, Kiral sending rapid-fire directions. They knew the consulate's layout by heart, had drilled it two hundred times in the Descartes Room, but they did not know where the sword would be.

They had drilled what Hong claimed was the most efficient path through the consulate but coming in through the atrium had flipped the cardinality.

Reina took over the chat from Kiral, coming in a bright fuchsia.

—I'm here with Hong. You got a conference room down the hall, and a suite of offices beside that. Start there, then go up one story to check the archives.

Reina ran another program, and now a faint orange schematic of the consulate flickered into the lower right quadrant of Ben's vision, with each of them represented by a color-coded dot. When he moved his eyes towards the image it zoomed in to show a more detailed view of the floor plan. As they proceeded, their course was tracked as a series of minute dashed lines.

They proceeded methodically, fanning out to open every drawer, every cabinet. They looked under every table, desk and chair, behind every piece of art and tapestry, in every flowerpot and stairwell.

From time to time, Reina, now tapped into the security system from the inside, and thus capable of seeing the motion of the consulate's skeleton crew of guards, would alert them to movement.

—Turn around. You gotta do the long way or hide your asses.

Every time they left a room empty-handed, Ben's eyes would flicker to the mocking countdown clock in its inexorable march towards zero.

After the first ten minutes, during which they passed through the first floors of three adjoining townhouses, he began to grow impatient.

After the second ten minutes, angry.

After the twenty-third minute, the feeling of panic that until that point he had managed to stave off, became more than he could bear.

—What the hell is going on, Amina? You said the sword was here.

They were in the kitchens now, and Amina had gone into the walk-in refrigerator to see whether the sword was stashed in that unlikeliest of places. Ben could see her through the door, standing on an overturned milk crate on her tiptoes, reaching behind the jars of pickles and tubs of vegetables to feel around on the upper shelf.

She spelled her answer one-handed:
—It is.
—Don't worry, Alejandrx tried to assure him.
—Worry? I'm panicking!

Kiral sent a note over the transom:
—Mr. Nakamura is not wrong to worry about the timing.

Amina emerged from the fridge. Amina was still for a long time. Ben wondered, irrationally, whether they were communicating telepathically.

Then, a moment later, Amina said: —I think we should split up.

Alejandrx: —No. Too dangerous.

Ben, anxious and eager, agreed with Amina. —We can cover twice as much ground!

Kiral chimed in through the chat: —I can direct Amina while Reina covers you two.

Ben waited for Alejandrx to respond. Impossible to know what shx was thinking behind the mask. Even hxr body language was unreadable. At last, shx gave a curt nod of hxr head.

Amina reached out and placed a hand on each of their shoulders.

—The sword is here, Mr. Nakamura. I guarantee it.

She gave their shoulders a squeeze, and in another moment she was gone.

ONE OF THE townhomes had been reserved as a pied a terre for the Villaseñor family, complete with wine cellar, an indoor bocce court, and a vast nursery with accompanying quarters for the army of governesses for Villaseñor's nine children.

It was here that Ben and Alejandrx found themselves. Five minutes on the clock.

Ben was glad not to be alone. There were ten times the cabinets, drawers, and crannies, any one of which would have provided a hiding place for the blade.

Alejandrx moved quickly but without urgency. From time to time, shx would signal through the chat that they were coming up empty-handed. Hong, who had taken over for Reina, could do little but urge them to keep moving.

—I just had a thought, Ben said.

He was raising the mattresses in the twins' cribs, just the length of the sword in its scabbard.

—What?

—What if the blade is in security? It's the only room with a constant armed presence.

Alejandrx was beside a wide lacquered white dresser, rifling through the drawers. Shx stared at Ben for fifteen seconds. The countdown timer told him.

—We can try there last.

Just then Amina pinged them.

—I've no good news, but I did find the server room.

Ben's heart palpitated. Had he been so inclined, he could have toppled his rival with a few strategic drives of even the replica blade. Better still, he had the decryptor. Amina did, at any rate. He little doubted he could have accessed Villaseñor's entire security network. With enough time he might even have shut it down.

Who knew what such a move would precipitate? He tingled with dread to imagine.

—Ben?

Alejandrx was at the doorway. He shook himself from his reverie. The countdown was drawing dangerously low. The back of his throat was acrid with bile, and despite the suit, Ben felt himself beginning to sweat.

Alejandrx, for all hxr surface calm, picked up the pace. Ben did his best to free ride on hxr energy. Shx seemed to glide across the floor, hxr shoulders loose, unperturbed.

It was impossible. It was harder and harder to control his thoughts, and he grew increasingly agitated. He felt his hands would not obey him. More than once he had lost his grip on door handles, dresser knobs.

Where was the damned sword?

Amina had sworn that the sword was there. He had staked the survival of the clan on the power of her promises. He did not want to curdle into distrust. To give up that trust was to admit he was a fool.

They were in the master bedroom when Amina's text appeared in the dialogue.

—Ale, something is—

And then Amina disappeared. The green dot, which Ben had tracked half-consciously through the rendering of the consulate simply blinked off.

Alejandrx saw too. Shx sank to a crouch, began to sign furiously.

—Kiral! Hong! Where is Amina? We've lost contact.

Neither Kiral nor Hong responded. A moment later the entire feed failed: the building specs, the countdown timer, the chat, the readouts. The world, which until that moment had glowed in digitally-enhanced light, went dark.

Ben and Alejandrx turned to take one another in. Shx raised a single finger to her apparatus, tapped it. A question. Could he breathe? Ben nodded. Good thing Kiral was not measuring his heart rate now.

Alejandrx indicated that they should find some place to hide, regroup. There: the walk-in closet. Ben ran, the blood pounding so loudly in his ears, he mistook it for footsteps. In the closet, lined from wall to wall with pairs of gorgeous shoes, oxblood leather and gleaming buckles, he started to pull the mask from his face, but Alejandrx took his hands and stopped him. Shx took his belt and gave it a shake. His first thought was, here? It took another moment to realize that shx was hard wiring them together. Shx adjusted a switch on his belt and the suit began to glow, faintly.

A moment later, most of their systems were operational. The 3-D rendering of the consulate blinked into place. Amina's dot was still missing.

The countdown clock returned too, and with it the chat function, bringing a barrage from Hong and Kiral.

—There you are!

—What the hell is going on there?!

Alejandrx began to sign. —We need to find Amina.

Kiral: —I have no bead on her. We lost you all at once.

Hong: —It's highly unusual for all three systems to fail at once.

—We're running on the auxiliary. Ben is charging.

—Amina would know to do that, too.

—Where was she when you lost her?

—Wait!

Ben had to stop himself from stamping his foot.

—What we need to find is the sword.

Alejandrx stood before him now, unmoving as a statue. Had shx stiffened? They were inches apart, literally connected by wire, yet shx could have been ten thousand miles away for all that he could fathom what was in hxr heart. It was hard enough to understand what was in his own.

He was struck suddenly by the callousness of what he had said. He was glad that he was masked.

—It was wrong of me to say that. Go for her. I will meet you at the rendezvous.

—We do not have much time.

—All the more reason to separate. I know the consulate by heart. There isn't much else to search.

Alejandrx disconnected the hardwire. It spiraled back into its slot with a whirr.

Shx closed the little space between them, placed hxr hand against his chin. Then, quickly, almost impatiently, shx turned and unclasped the sword's crosswise belt from hxr chest. The scabbard slipped but Ben was there to grab it. Shx took it from his hands, reached behind him. In a moment he felt the unfamiliar stiffness of the sheath against his upper back. Shx clicked the buckle into place. It closed with a hollow tick that seemed to fill the consulate.

Ben took hxr hand, pulled hxr close to him. For a moment they simply touched one another, hxr hands moving across his chest, his own against hxr hips, the small of hxr lower back.

It was shx who drew away.

BEN WATCHED THE red dot of Alejandrx's avatar move through the map like a ghost passing through walls. Hxr concern for Amina was palpable.

Ben gave Amina very little thought. If the suits were this temperamental—a fact which annoyed him, more than anything—it was most likely she had simply come across a dead zone, some place in the consulate that prevented her from being in contact with the network. A vault? A cellar? A safe? She may even have stumbled upon the sword.

At that possibility, he found his frustration and distrust beginning to mount. Was it truly only circumstance that he was now alone, and still no sign of the sword?

As if in answer to that recurrent question, there was a sudden piercing shriek in his earpiece, so loud he fell to his knees, crying out in pain. The bug suit went completely dead.

Without the vision enhancement, he could not see. He signed a few times, desperate for a response, but there was nothing.

The bug suit was suddenly suffocating, blinding, deafening. He clawed the breathing apparatus free, greedily gulping down the cool air. He strained to listen for the others. Did he hear footsteps?

His mind raced to catch up. No way the suit had simply failed. Someone must have triggered an EMP.

Someone? Who? The guards?

Amina?

To his dismay, he heard running footsteps. He did some quick mental calculations. He knew where Alejandrx had been when the suit failed—too far for the footsteps to be hxrs.

They must belong to the guards, which meant that they had heard him cry out.

Why hadn't Hong told him they were close enough to pursue?

Ben's heart sank as the reality of their failure set in. They had come all this way for nothing. He didn't need the countdown clock to know the mission was aborted. The only thing to do now was to escape. He could only hope that Amina had somehow found the sword, though he knew deep down that his suspicions had been borne out.

He reflected bitterly that at least he knew his escape route well. They had drilled it for so many hours in the warehouse. All he could do now was get away.

twenty four

BEN PAUSED FOR a moment. The blood was pounding in his ears, so it took a moment before he heard—yes, more footsteps. Two sets, ever so slightly syncopated.

He held his breath. They were nearby, low, the sounds not of heavy boots but of people trying to move quietly.

To his surprise, he felt neither rage nor disappointment, but joy. He had found them! Now all he needed was to catch up. They were directly overhead, moving north. He scanned his mental map. They were in a corridor of spacious open-plan office space. He knew the nearest junction between their story and his was a stairwell. He followed the sounds of their movement, moving as quietly as he could, surprised by how utterly depleted he was. They were moving very quickly.

He thought he might catch them up at the stairwell, but he found when he reached it that the footsteps were gone. He strained to listen. Could they possibly have gone upstairs? Why would they?

There they were again! Nearer than he had dared to hope. He wanted to cry out for them to wait for him, but the thought could go no further.

All at once their pace picked up, and Ben broke into a flat-out sprint through the final building, past glass-walled conference rooms, a kitchenette with an espresso machine, a wall sign indicating the consulate's pool and fitness center.

He followed the footsteps where he knew they must now lead: the atrium. This was not the rendezvous. This was adaptation.

He stopped in the doorway, glanced down at the security box, now divested of their network override. Even now, the mission failed, they were erasing all signs of their presence.

Ben took a few steps along the slatted wooden path that wound between the trees. He stared up into the ink-black hole of the atrium's opening.

That was where his heart fell out of his body.

There in the blackness, staring down at him from the rooftop were two red eyes, two green.

There was a sudden rushing vortex of sound, a low rumble that rattled his bones and sent the nesting birds into hysterics. A modified VTOL, glossy black, unmarked, descended from the night sky, its head beams slashing through the atrium's ironwork, bathing the interior with ribbons of sharp white light.

It came to a stop just above the opening, and the thrust of its rotor blades caused every leaf and branch to quake. The roosting birds went berserk, screaming maniacally as they tried to escape through the arboretum ceiling, only to find themselves violently buffeted back.

On the machine, a glinting door slid aside and first one then the other black figure took hold of the side and swung up into its belly.

Just as the VTOL began to pull away, Ben saw the red-eyed figure lean from the doorway, lean so far that he knew shx must be lashed in. Hxr hands moved in the darkness, making the same sign again and again until the VTOL banked and disappeared into the blackness of the night.

Benjiro saw enough to know shx said, "I'm sorry."

twenty five

Because it was his ascension, the convocation of the clans was hosted in the Nakamura sinecure, north of the city at the Hyde Park estate, where once long-ago Franklin Delano Roosevelt had kept home.

For hours the families of the other clans had been arriving in the full formal regalia of the cyberstate oligarchy: long faux-fur-lined robes, veils, saris, kimonos. The materials were expensive, gorgeous, the styles a perfect pastiche of the past and the sensibilities of the bleeding edge. The fashion was matched only by the hair and makeup, elaborate and striking and beautiful.

The regents wore swords in honor of the occasion.

Clan Nakamura had spared no expense. There were crates of champagne, acres of hors d'ouvres on long white-linen-clad tables. Grass tennis courts and croquet pitches had been laid out for the children. An army of caterers and waiters thronged like ants between the gardens, the fields, the great hall and the kitchens.

Ben had seen none of it. He had retreated to his chambers at first light, as was the custom, and would not be called until the formal opening of the ceremony.

He was supposed to spend the time in quiet reflection. He had spent it in a knot of panic and exasperation.

There was a small irony in the fact that the year of his ascension would be the only time he was not there. As scion, and later as regent, he would attend until his own scion came of age. Benjiro Nakamura VI, his father, was not a communicative man, but it had become clear that he was tired of the responsibilities of regency, and trusted that his investments in his son's education and manners had sufficiently prepared him for his turn in the maw.

Ben wondered, too, whether his father knew he wasn't very good at what he did. It had been forced on him, as it had been forced on his own father. His real passion was sailing.

Ben went to the west-facing window. The sun was low in the sky. It wouldn't be long before the convocation began.

Unlike his guests, Ben was dressed in simple attire: dark suit, plum slippers. His hair was held back in a tight topknot, bound with a strip of silk from his late mother's wedding dress which his sister Sumaya had given to him that morning. He had been touched.

The ersatz Matsukata rested in its scabbard at the foot of the bed.

Ben could not imagine what was to come.

EVEN AS THE sound of the VTOL faded away, Ben had faced the bitter truth of Amina's betrayal. It was not hard; a part of him had been prepared for this since before he knew her.

Whatever it was she had really wanted from him, she had orchestrated things to end this way. She—really, all of them—must have known that because of his position, had he been discovered at the consulate, the episode would be erased from the formal record for the sake of preserving the peace between the sinecures.

Or perhaps they simply did not care what happened to him.

Which meant that Alejandrx did not care…

Except Alejandrx had left a rope dangling from the aperture in the ceiling. If he could make it to the roof, he might be able to stick to the original plan.

He went to the rope, gave it a tug. It was still tightly affixed to the winch. Ben took a few deep breaths. He was strong enough, well-trained enough, to make it to the top if his nerves held. He gripped the rope in both hands and tried to hoist himself up.

He pulled himself an arm's length up, then another.

He could not sustain it. The knowledge that shx had left him here—he no longer cared what happened to him. Let Villaseñor find him here, stranded, a fool on an impossible mission.

Retrieve the sword? What in God's name had he been thinking? He had been so stupid to have reached out to Amina. So gullible to have believed even for a moment that she would be true to her word. He remembered with fury the way she had looked into his eyes and said to him, directly to his face, that, "The sword will be there. I swear on my honor."

Rage was a better fuel than fear. He was not a man to be so easily crossed. He would find them, one by one, and he would make them pay.

He took the rope again in his hands. This time he climbed with the assurance of a man who did not know defeat.

In a minute he was on the roof. He decided to leave the rope and grapple. Give Villaseñor something to chew over. He wondered—hoped—that someone had seen the VTOL. His escape now depended on it.

Ben made his way quickly back along the pergola. He scaled the final column, backtracked along the pathway they had taken upon their arrival. At last, he came to the long flat expanse of the kitchens, through which he had passed just ten minutes before. Beside them were the dumpsters where they were supposed to wait and hide. There was a sliding plastic doorway on the side of the nearest dumpster. Ben slipped it open, hoisted himself a final time, and leapt through the hole.

He barely had time to slide the door closed before the sheer nightmare of the smells overtook him, a hideous melange of soiled diapers, rotting fish, rancid food, and mold. The garbage was up to his chest, and he pushed his way through it, slipping with each step as he plodded towards the far wall.

He pulled the bug mask desperately down over his face. It was hard to breathe with the suit dead, and the heat of the suit and the garbage was oppressive, but the mask helped to block the smell, and that was enough. He lasted as long as he could on a series of shallow breaths, before sneaking a deep and putrid breath to fill his lungs.

He braced himself to wait. There was nothing else to do. For a long time, he waited standing in the garbage, but at the sound of voices, he forced himself to sink into the filth, first up to the neck and then, at the terrible sound of the plastic door being slid aside, fully underneath a sloping pile of garbage.

"Anything?"

"Christ, no."

He waited there until his lungs burned, then forced himself to wait longer still.

The voices continued to speak, though he could no longer make out what they said.

Then to his horror the dumpster began to vibrate. "What the hell?"

"It's automated. There's a trigger from the barge. Just get out of the way. And close that fucking door. Jesus."

At last, Ben pushed himself out of the garbage. To his relief, the door was closed. The dumpster continued to rattle and thump. There was a sudden stop, then a terrible lurch and in a moment, Ben found himself sliding rapidly along the wall, sloshing among the bags and their vile emanations into a sudden splash of oily yellow light.

He landed painfully on his knee and back, the fall broken only because he landed on a mountain of garbage.

He lay still until he felt the electric thrum of the air change as the barge decoupled from the sea wall's electromagnet. He slipped and slid his way out of the garbage, across the length of the barge, and pulled himself up onto the roof of the engine room. He tore the mask from his face, retched into the river, and collapsed.

He knew that eventually he would be floated down the coast to a landfill in Pennsylvania. He supposed that he could scale the sea wall at any of the barge's stops, but as the city drifted by, he was relieved that he had time to think.

It was only then that he recalled that his phone was tucked into a zippered pocket on his vest. He had not used it for so long that he had forgotten that it existed. He retrieved it now and powered it on.

It took a moment, but as it found a network signal, it began to tremble, as thousands of notifications, pings, calls, voicemails, emails, and texts caught up with him. It rattled for so long and with such mechanical regularity that he caught himself barking an ironic laugh.

He would clear things up in time. There was only one person he needed now, his chargé d'affairs. Ben pulled up her name from his expanding list of missed calls.

Amina was not the only one, after all, with access to a VTOL.

twenty

All that remained was to see what Villaseñor had planned for the ceremony.

Had he already begun to spread the word among the regents, so that his would not be the sole voice of protest when Benjiro's right to rule was put to the peers?

There was a sudden buzz from the dresser where Ben had set aside his phone. He went to check the message, wondering who it could possibly be. Everyone he knew would be at the convocation.

Not everyone. There was a message on the UI for the dark web forum through which he'd first reached out to Amina.

—Congratulations on your ascension to regency. You must be very pleased.

Ben typed furiously back: —What do you want?

—Payment for services rendered.

—Is this some kind of sick joke?
—I promised you the sword. I have kept my promise.
He started to type: *You lie.*

He did not hit send. He could never truly have the last word. He did not want her intrusion to spoil his day. As if her betrayal were not enough.

For the thousandth time, Ben went to the sword, drawing it from the scabbard. It truly was astonishing. Every fiber of the stitching on the handle had been reproduced. The balance, the weight of the thing was perfect…

Ben tilted the sword in the light to inspect Madrid's engraving: マドリッド etched into the mune, just above the scabbard collar, so small it could be mistaken for a scratch. Not so incredible to imagine a bit of wear on an eight-hundred-year-old sword. He could feign ignorance of the forgery…

What was it Madrid had called it?

Magic.

Ben ran his finger along Madrid's absurd addition. *Madoriddo.* Ben knitted his brow. He had liked the man. All part of the act, he supposed. The misdirection.

What he could not recall was whether Matsukata had engraved his own name on the Nakamura Matsukata. It was an idle thought, but he really ought to know.

The misdirection…

Ben's heart began to race. With shaking hands, he drew out six inches of Matsukata's blade.

There, just above the habaki, Madrid's name. Ben ran his finger over it. Then, with his fingernail he began to scratch at it. It took a minute, but he found the edge of the micro-thin sticker. Once loosened, it peeled off with a single tug. There, enclosed in a filmy rectangle of adhesive, was Matsukata's name in minute script:

松方

The remnants of Madrid's sleight of hand was stuck to his finger.
The sword will be there. On my honor.
She was brilliant, simply brilliant.
Ben began to laugh.

EPILOGUE

BEN RETURNED TO his phone.
—Damn you, Amina. I see it. I'm beyond relief.
There was a minute before she responded.
—I'm glad there are no hard feelings. The terms of our contract have been met. You have the sword. I require payment.
—You stole it!
—I arranged for it to be stolen. Inartful, I believe you said. Not the same thing.
—Why should I pay you?
—Because you have the sword.
Ben laughed. His relief was absolute. He felt generous.
—I'll do it now.
He toggled over to the dark web. Unlike his father, Ben had always had a head for numbers. A teenage interest in the banking system had inspired him to stockpile a substantial amount of cash in a nesting doll of shell companies scattered throughout the rival sinecures. Part of his interest had been in a form of low-grade financial warfare. His wealth was so vast that in the smaller sinecures, a withdrawal from one of his accounts could spur a drop in the value of the local currency and a concomitant run on the banks.

He had long ago mapped out the flow of payments to Amina to be as little disruptive as possible. He executed the series of transactions now, sending the money into the accounts Amina proffered to him through the UI. He knew intimately how clever she could be. No forensic accountant would ever track her down.

He was supposed to be meditating on his future. He found that closing this chapter was helping to calm his nerves.

He had the sword. Had never truly lost it.

The thought gave him pause. He blinked several times as hot tears stung his eyes. He knew he had lost something far more precious.

—I need to ask you a question.

For a long time Amina did not respond.

—This is Kiral. What?

—Why? Why steal the sword?

—Are you really so daft, Nakamura? After all that?

—I may be.

There was no response.

Was it for the bounty? Too simple, and in that case why the con? Why not demand the ransom money and be done with it? What did they get out of stringing him along for two…

There was a low knock on his door.

"One moment."

He set the phone aside and went to the door. His chargé was there. She was Black, Eritrean by descent, dressed in slim fawn slacks and a dark green velvet jacket. Her hair was platinum, her eyes bright behind her glasses.

"They're ready for you, sir."

"Help me with the scabbard."

She followed him into the room. They worked together to affix the saya to his left side, snug in the obi, blade side up.

"Is Villaseñor arrived?"

"He's the last of them. I think the others were starting to get bored."

Ben had always liked Naomi. She had little patience for fuss.

"How do I look?"

"You look the part. How are you feeling?"

"I'm not sure."

"You were born for it, sir."

On an impulse, he leaned forward and hugged her. When he drew back, her smile was genuine.

He followed her downstairs, through discreet back corridors, out of sight of the guests, who had begun to make their way inside as the sun set and the outdoor air cooled.

The regents had convened in the library.

His father had told him nothing about his own ascension, so Ben knew very little about the ceremony. He only knew that, despite the opulence of the surroundings, the actual convocation had a private, almost secretive quality to it.

At the door to the library, Naomi stopped. She rapped at the door, which was opened by another chargé, an older man with a trim white goatee. He beckoned them inside.

The other regents were there, dressed in their finery, swords at their hips. They stood in pairs or threes, talking of business and grandchildren.

Leonard Spitz, the eldest of them, was leaning against an armchair reading a leather-bound novel. His chargé had to tap his shoulder to alert him to Ben's presence. When he saw the man of the hour, he snapped the book shut and set it aside. He indicated with a clearing of the throat that the others should take their seats at the long oak table that ran the length of the library.

Ben remained standing while the others settled in. The chargé discretely took their exit, and Ben was left alone with the regents of the clans. He had met these men at other convocations through the years and had gone to school with their sons and brothers. Still, they were strangers to him.

Even his father, conspicuous without the Nakamura Matsukata by his side, happier behind the eyes than Ben could recall ever seeing him. He had brought a long-stemmed glass of wine into the library with him, and he set it down at the foot of the table. Spitz, as the elder statesman, had taken the head.

"Are we all here?"

There was a murmur of assent. Ben cast his eyes around the table. He had not yet seen Villaseñor—never mind, there he was.

Ben reflected for a moment on the man's innocence. He had been so sure that it was he who had taken the sword. His mind raced, from embarrassment at his mistake, to elation—for had he not bested the dot knot? Was his rival aware of the breach? Did he know anything at all about the night in the consulate?

And then it hit him, so obvious as to make him dizzy. He'd spent two weeks untethered from the world, cracking the uncrackable...

Spitz again cleared his throat and began to invoke the ceremony. Ben wasn't listening.

There was a noise from outside the library, the sound of running and voices raised. Spitz heard it too and lost his train of thought. Scowling, he indicated to his chargé that he should ensure they were not interrupted.

He began again.

"Benjiro Ibn Benjiro Ayad Nakamura, scion of clan Nakamura and regent-ascendant of the Nakamura cybersinecure, steward of the Nakamura Matsukata—"

At this, Ben drew the blade from its scabbard, holding it aloft. There were murmurs of assent and admiration from the other regents. They knew its history; its power.

There was a rap at the door, and Spitz, who had continued with the invocation, lost his place again.

"Confound it, who is it?"

The door opened. Villaseñor's chargé came quickly into the room, and, ignoring the icy stares of the others, went directly to his regent's side to whisper in his ear.

Villaseñor's face went grey. He tried to rise from his chair, but his knees were too weak.

"Forgive me, it's—"

But he could not even say the words. His chargé rose from where he had been kneeling.

"The sinecure's security apparatus has been disabled."

There was a general swell of shock as the realization of what this could mean spread.

The bubble moment of the convocation had popped. The library doors were flung open, and panic-stricken guests began to seek out the regents.

Ben caught Naomi's eye, beckoned her over.

"What do you know?"

"Only that there's some kind of crisis."

"Public?"

"It would appear so."

"The banquet hall. Dim the lights. Sync my phone—no, yours—with the audio system."

Naomi nodded and slipped away.

Across the room, Ben caught his father's eye. The old man smiled and shrugged, as if to say, "You wanted the damned thing—now it's yours!"

Ben urged everyone to make their way to the banquet hall, where they would learn together what was going on.

Out of the corner of his eye, he could make out Villaseñor slumped over in his seat, his chargé still beside him, fanning him with a book. Villaseñor's wife, tall and striking, with ink black hair in plaits, dressed in the bright red traditional dress of her native Jalisco, stood behind him, gripping his shoulder as if it was the only thing between herself and annihilation.

His guests had begun to move. Ben caught up one of his servants and directed him to spread the word that everyone should be corralled into banquet hall.

Two minutes later, it was done. Naomi had linked to the sound system and was projecting the news in holographic 3-D from her phone onto the near wall. Ben did not bother to call for quiet.

The view was taken from a helicopter, showing tens, even hundreds of thousands thronging the streets of Ciudad de México. The noise of the crowd, even at that distance, was deafening.

The helicopter banked, flying closer to what had once been the Presidential Palace, but was now the seat of Villaseñor's cybersinecure.

Or was it?

Ben glanced at Villaseñor, now seated in a chair at the far wall of the banquet hall. The man's eyes were locked on the screen, his expression a blend of bafflement and despair.

Ben's eyes flickered back to the news broadcast. There was a figure on the balcony overlooking the crowds.

Now another person came out to join them.

The helicopter drew closer still. Ben gasped.

It was Amina. She was dressed formally, in a dark cherry pant suit and cream-colored blouse. Big gold hoops hung from her ears. She was beaming, waving at the crowd.

Kiral was beside her, their hands clenched upon the balcony railing. Once or twice, they raised their joined hands, to approving roars from the crowds.

"Who is she?"

"What on earth is going on?"

Ben turned again to Villaseñor, who could only shake his head. "I've no idea. I've never seen the woman before, I swear it."

A woman's voice cut in over the feed.

"Reports are coming in from Ciudad de México that a group of democratic rebels has successfully orchestrated a bloodless coup against the Villaseñor sinecure. Regent Villaseñor is out of the sinecure to attend the ascension ceremony of Benjiro Ibn Benjiro Ayad Nakamura of the Manahatta Sinecure. Sources say that the group breached and completely disabled Villaseñor's security apparatus, and that rebel sympathizers within the sinecure's bureaucracy moved immediately to depose Villaseñor's top administrators."

"No one is reported to have been killed," the correspondent continued. "At the news of the coup, the population of the Ciudad de México has thronged the streets in a surprising show of support for the leader whose name we are just now learning is…forgive me…Amina Adeyemi. I am being told that she is about to speak. Let's cut to that audio now."

The camera stabilized on a shot of Amina at the edge of the balcony. She raised her hands, held them aloft, and the crowd noise began to settle.

"Free citizens!"

There was a roar of joy from the crowd.

"Today is a glorious day, for on this day, for the first time in a century, the continent of North America is home once more to a democratic nation."

The noise from the crowd was so loud it caused the banquet hall to tremble.

Amina raised her hand again.

"In three months' time, we will host free and fair elections to determine the leadership of our new country."

Ben's heart, which had been fluttering as the slow realization of the vastness of Amina's undertaking came into view, began to pound.

Onto the balcony, to stand with their leader, had come the others: Dmitri Madrid, Reina Acevedo, Patrick Hong, Irina Moiseyev. There were others there, too, faces unfamiliar to Ben, but whose commitment to Amina and to her cause he could begin to understand.

He scanned the crowd, searching now for the only face that mattered.

There shx was, pushing hxr way to the front to stand alongside hxr companions.

Amina continued to speak, but her words were inaudible now against the din of the crowd.

Alejandrx had spotted the helicopter. Shx turned hxr face to it and raised hxr hands.

—I am sorry. It was real. But so is this.

acknowledgments

I WANT TO begin by thanking Mike Swain for reading the first short story draft of this novella and telling me, in so many words, "I want more." Thanks to my other readers, Asher Lack and Mark Jacobs. I'm eternally grateful to dave, who took a gamble on the book. Thank you for both the editorial eye and the conversations.

There is no one to whom I am more grateful than Brianne. The deepest reader I have ever known, sounding board to all my ideas, and midwife to the best of them. You have believed in my writing even when I have not believed in it myself. Anything I have been able to say about love, I have been able to say because I love you.

author's note

QUOTATIONS FROM THE Plutarch are from https://penelope.uchicago.edu/Thayer/E/Roman/Texts/Plutarch/Lives/Alexander*/3.html

This book was written and edited in its entirety on my phone while putting my children to sleep.

about the author

Thomas Bulen Jacobs was raised overseas, in Latin America, Turkey and Spain. He is a graduate of the Great Books program at St. John's College in Annapolis, and the author of a dozen short stories. He lives with his wife and family in Massachusetts.

about the press

Neon Hemlock is a Washington, DC-based small press publishing speculative fiction, rad zines, and queer chapbooks. Publishers Weekly once called us "the apex of queer speculative fiction publishing" and we're still beaming. Learn more about us at neonhemlock.com and on social medias at @neonhemlock.

www.ingramcontent.com/pod-product-compliance
Lightning Source LLC
LaVergne TN
LVHW040058080526
838202LV00045B/3689